Captive
Planet

Captive Planet

GREGORY J. SMITH

BETHANY HOUSE PUBLISHERS
MINNEAPOLIS, MINNESOTA 55438
A Division of Bethany Fellowship, Inc.

Published by Bethany House Publishers
A Division of Bethany Fellowship, Inc.
6820 Auto Club Road, Minneapolis, Minnesota 55438

Printed in the United States of America

Library of Congress Cataloging-in-Publication Data

Smith, Gregory J. (Gregory Jon)
    Captive planet.

    (Star quest books)
    I. Title.   II. Series.
PS3569.M5357C36   1986   813'.54   86–8252
ISBN 0–87123–868–3 (pbk.)

To the dear friends who assisted with
the writing of this book; especially to
my wife, Rebecca Ann, for nudging,
encouraging and assisting in so many ways.

GREGORY JON SMITH, a sci-fi buff since his teen years, has combined his love for the genre with his skill as a professional writer. A graduate from the University of Minnesota, he worked as the publications director for Lutherans for Life for a number of years, has written several articles for community newspapers and has been a contributing editor to *Debate* magazine. CAPTIVE PLANET is his first book.

Chapter One

He paused in the doorway to search the darkness. The odor drifting up to his nostrils caused him to momentarily wonder at the wisdom of entering the tavern. It smelled like every other spaceport inn. Cleanliness was obviously not important to the owner—nor to most of his clientele.

Lam Laeo preferred order; as he entered, the sight of the place depressed him. Looking for an open table, he mentally noted the others in the room: port mechanics, crew members on ship leave, some locals and shadowy figures in a distant corner.

Lam, in contrast, was neatly dressed in flight pants and a tunic. The hood rested on his shoulders, exposing nicely trimmed sandy hair. The tunic kindly concealed a slight weight problem. Although Lam tried to keep trim, there was little opportunity for exercise on his small craft in zero gravity.

Lam finally located a free table and sat down. As he waited for service, he gazed blankly toward the wall, oblivious to the clatter and conversation around him in the room. His green eyes focused on nothing except when he would occasionally twist around to glance at the door. The only other noticeable movement was his almost subconscious pat on something concealed beneath his tunic.

A voice behind startled him out of his reverie.

"House?" grunted the tavern-keeper in *Common*, the trade language of most spaceports.

"That'll be fine," answered Lam.

"Twenty *demas*," announced the tavern-keeper, handing Lam a dirty-looking glass full of the house drink, a pungent brew made from roots native to Saan, and wiping a fat hand on his grimy apron to prepare for the transaction.

"Twenty demas?" protested Lam. "I've gotten better prices from pirates!" The tavern-keeper just stared belligerently, his hand under Lam's nose. Normally Lam would have pressed the matter—the small insignia on his tunic indicated membership in the Interstellar Merchants Union, so he was used to arguing for a fair price. But Lam was fatigued. He dug out the necessary coins. The tavern-keeper grabbed them and turned away, muttering grumpily at having been challenged.

Lam began to feel better as the drink warmed him from the damp chill outside. *The Redlyn deal went well*, he mused. He could now buy new supplies for *Starjumper*. He might even be able to buy paint for the ship's hull tiles. They were starting to look scarred, and Lam did not want people wondering how they got that way. *Besides, a good impression is good for business*, he noted.

Taking another sip, his daydreaming envisioned a welcomed night of sleeping in gravity for a change.

A raspy voice disrupted his musings. "License!" the voice demanded. Lam knew it was a Redlyn pistol pressed against his back. He also knew the voice belonged to a Doomen soldier. Lam shivered every time he heard a Doomen voice, like the rattle in the throat of a dying man.

"Sure," muttered Lam, reaching into one of his pockets for the foil-embossed card emblazoned with the seal of the Dominion. He slowly turned to hand it to the soldier. It wouldn't do to startle him. The Doomen accepted the card with his free gloved hand. He did not look at the card.

Lam stared into the Doomen's face. The head carried a helmet of the same black, padded material that armored the body. The helmet covered the top half of his face except for the half-circles cut for the eyes. Lam, however, could not see the Doomen's eyes—only darkness. Lam remembered tavern tales that reported Doomen had no eyes; they sensed everything with their minds.

The Doomen's black-gloved hand fingered the license, his face still directed toward Lam. Lam's uneasiness grew with each moment of silence.

"Your business on Saan?" rasped out the Doomen.

Lam's heart was beating so hard he wondered fleetingly if the Doomen noticed. Their presence often evoked irrational fear in people, but knowing this did not calm Lam's alarm.

"I just delivered a kreln of Redlyn crystals to the freighter Diadem," answered Lam, attempting to keep control of his voice.

"You are Redlyn licensed?"

"Of course. It's on my license." The Dominion had never grilled him like this at any port.

"Others on ship?" demanded the Doomen relentlessly.

"No. I work alone," answered Lam. He was now silently reviewing math tables, trying to keep his mind off his own Redlyn pistol concealed under his tunic. Lam had heard rumors (which he now fervently hoped were groundless) that the Doomen could read minds. The Dominion had banned all private weapons; the Doomen alone were assigned to keep the peace in the galaxy and carry pistols.

The black figure handed Lam his license and turned away. Lam breathed out slowly as he let down his guard—exactly what the Doomen expected. In a lightning move, he swung back and ripped Lam's tunic with the sharpened handle of his pistol, the other hand was grasping for Lam's weapon.

Without a conscious decision, Lam planted his fist in the Doomen's face. He staggered back a couple of steps and dropped Lam's pistol. When Lam reached down for it with his good hand (the other felt as though it had been broken against the Doomen's face), the soldier swung a metal-tipped boot against Lam's skull. Though not well-aimed, the blow sent Lam to the floor holding his head in pain.

As the Doomen carefully raised his own pistol and took aim at Lam, a bolt of light flashed through the room, momentarily blinding the stunned onlookers whose eyes were accustomed to the tavern's dimness. Astonished, Lam blinked hard twice and looked at the floor in front of him. Someone else had fired first. The Doomen soldier lay in several smoldering parts at Lam's feet.

Like a broken holograph, everyone in the tavern sat in dazed silence, staring at Lam and the remains of one of the Dominion's elite. The pounding and ringing in Lam's ears came from within.

The shadows in the corner of the tavern had concealed a tall figure. He now emerged, tucking a pistol beneath his tunic.

"Friend," Lam barely heard the figure call through the ringing. *Friend*? Lam wondered through his mental fog. *I've never seen him before.* As the stranger approached, Lam noticed that he was a large man with trim build, dressed in planet-side trousers and a tunic with its hood raised. A simple amulet around his neck caught the tavern lights. In the dimness, Lam could not distinguish the man's features.

"Friend," repeated the man. He spoke in Common, but with an accent Lam could not place. "You must leave here. Come with me." The man turned and stepped briskly toward a service door.

"W-wait a minute," protested Lam, still sitting in a daze on the floor.

His rescuer turned and said quickly but calmly, his voice low, "Perhaps you do not know that when one Doomen is killed, the others nearby know about it instantly. There are many near. We have only moments—" The man interrupted himself and glanced at the tavern door. Lam did the same but neither saw nor heard anything. Grabbing Lam's arm, the stranger pulled the bewildered merchant to his feet. Lam grabbed his pistol from the floor and hesitantly followed the tall figure through the service door and out into the blackened alley.

As Lam left, everyone in the tavern eyed him. In spite of his narrow escape, he felt a momentary urge to say something clever. He stifled it.

Lam was instantly lost. The mysterious deliverer led him skillfully through back alleys and crawl spaces. Lam slipped twice on the slimy pavement, and in the dark could not find a handhold on the equally slime-covered walls beside him. Falling a third time with a thud, Lam's guide turned to help him back to his feet. Lam refused the outstretched hand, preferring to sit and catch his breath.

"You risked your life in there for me," said Lam between gasps. "What's in it for you?"

"What makes you think there's anything *in* it for me?" asked the stranger.

"Well," Lam hesitated, surprised by the question. "Why else would you save my life? You must have *some* reason."

The hooded man seemed to be looking down at him, studying him, although Lam could not be sure in the concealing darkness. After a long, silent pause, the man said, "Though you bear the Merchants' insignia, I suspect you are not a merchant—such a peaceful profession has little need of hidden weapons."

Astonished and alarmed, Lam groped for words to defend himself. Before he could collect his thoughts, the tall figure added, "Nor do merchants attack Doomen soldiers with so little cause; carrying weapons is not punishable by death, but assaulting a soldier is."

"You still have not told me who you are," demanded Lam, trying to change the conversation.

"Nor have you told me who you are," the stranger calmly answered. "For now that does not matter. Both of us are wanted by the Dominion and surrounded by Doomen anxious to avenge their comrade's death. We must act quickly." Turning to inspect their surroundings, he again resumed his swift pace down the foreboding alley.

Lam groaned and attempted to rub the cold sweat from his bewildered face. Forgetting the grim realities around him, he immediately regretted this move as his hand was covered with slime from the alley floor. A scaly creature ran across the other hand which held him propped up; he leaped to his feet with a disgusted grunt, shook his head in dismay and hurried after his disappearing guide.

Finally catching up, Lam found the stranger flattened up against the right hand wall, cautiously peering around the dimly lit corner. Lam decided the slimy muck on the wall was better than being discovered by a Doomen, and pressed himself tightly to it.

"My name is Padeus," whispered the hooded guide, "but most people call me 'Padu.' I am on a pilgrimage to the planet Tsu. And your name, my 'merchant' friend?"

"Lam," he offered, surprised that his companion had finally offered some information about himself. "Lam Laeo."

"We are just outside the port now, Lam—we must take your

ship to a place of refuge I know in the mountains outside the city. We will be safe there for a time."

"Wait a moment!" Lam protested. "Who put you in charge? How do you know about my ship? What kind of a place—"

Padu, still looking cautiously around the corner, held up his hand to quiet Lam. Acquiescing under protest, Lam muttered, "Well, I hope there is a decent landing pad."

The pair proceeded and reached the ship without detection. Lam knew that if they flew low to the ground and fast, they could escape detection in flight as well. The small planet was not a major port and did not possess sophisticated technology—only the best tracking equipment would be able to follow his ship. Yet, he shuddered at the thought of the Doomen's capabilities. His experience in the tavern had only confirmed his fears.

Strapped into Starjumper's pilot seat with Padu fastened into the seat beside him, Lam hurried through preflight proce- dures automatically, repeating over and over to himself, "Why is this happening to me?"

Quietly and quickly the ship lifted into the sky and sliced the atmosphere in the direction of the sanctuary Padu promised. The spaceport they left sat near the foothills of the mountains to which they were now flying. The planet Saan was mostly barren desert except near the base of the mountains where the clouds collided with the rocky cliffs and dropped their moisture. This made the port city cold and damp at night, and hot and steamy in the day. Saan had never been one of Lam's favorite stops. Reminded by the slimy stench he now carried, today Saan had become the least favorite. *What a stinking mess I'm in*, he thought.

They were soon in the safety of the mountains. No tracking gear could follow them here. Following Padu's instructions, Lam slowed the ship into a shallow, white-covered valley located high in the mountain range. Holding his breath, he maneuvered the craft between the jagged rocks that seemed to jut out of the mountain like teeth waiting for a tasty morsel. There was no landing pad—an unpleasant fact Lam noted with disgust; a coat of paint would never cover a rip in the hull from one of those monstrous rocks.

"We have friends here," Padu assured him.

"Terrific," mumbled Lam as he carefully guided the ship to a relatively smooth spot of smaller rocks. *No rips but plenty of scratches*, Lam groused to himself.

During the trip, Padu had pulled back his hood and Lam got his first good look at the man. He seemed old, very old, yet he possessed a young man's strength. His complexion was dark, with an olive tone, his features soft and his hair streaked with gray. Lam noticed the man was unusually tall, and wondered if the stranger had come from a small planet with low gravity.

Shutting off the ship's engines and systems, Lam opened a locker and took out a clean tunic to replace his filthy torn one. While exchanging, he discreetly checked his pistol. Escape from the Doomen soldier did not erase his present suspicions. Lam then moved to the ship's control panel and pressed a symbol; the portal swished open.

Steam rolled on the floor as the cold air from outside condensed the moisture from within. Regretfully glancing back at the warm, familiar interior of Starjumper, Lam took a deep breath and stepped down from the ship behind Padu.

Lam cursed as the white mass swallowed his leg up to his knee. *First slime, now snow.* "I hate snow," he growled. Lam pressed a device strapped to his wrist and the ship's portal closed. He stumbled after Padu, swearing when he fell in the snow.

"Hey! Would you mind telling me where we are going?" Lam shouted after Padu, who was already far ahead and managing to outdistance Lam through the unbroken snow.

No answer.

Lam shivered and struggled on, hoping it was not far.

About the time Lam was ready to shout to Padu that his feet were going numb, Padu stopped and waited. They had reached the first sign of habitation since landing—a snow-covered foot bridge that spanned a chasm and ended near the mouth of a cave. Starting across the bridge, Lam discovered that the wind blew harder through the chasm: it drove the cold through his tunic and tore at his nerves. The gusting wind forced Lam to grasp the ropes of the bridge tightly and at times to stop and huddle. Finally reaching solid ground, Lam was shaking from head to foot—the bitter cold and frazzled muscles had taken over. He staggered after Padu into the cave. As they penetrated the mountain, the cave looked increasingly like a man-made tunnel. A dim light ahead barely gave enough light to keep them from running into the walls. *At least its not slimy*, Lam noted sarcastically, then began to chuckle.

"Do you realize that I don't know anything about you except that you claim you're a pilgrim on your way to Tsu—a planet about which I know absolutely nothing?" asked Lam, his words echoing with his footsteps off the rough-hewn walls.

"Yes," said Padu. That was not the answer Lam wanted.

"Listen, Padu," he persisted. "It seems to me you were hiding in that tavern—I didn't see you when I came in. Obviously, it's not for my sake alone that we're on our way to hide out in this place, whatever it is. If you think I'm going to keep roaming this freezer-box with a fugitive, you'd better start talking. Now, what kind of pilgrim are you and why were you hiding?"

"Questions," said Padu with a laugh. "If I told you all I know, you might go back to the show. I can tell you only that we are approaching a secret colony established by a Tsuian ambassador."

"Why a secret colony?" Lam probed. "What are they hiding from?"

"Not everyone enjoys the Dominion's rule. You should know that."

The tunnel was getting lighter, and the wind blowing against the two was no longer cold. Lam breathed it in deeply. What at first sounded like the wind whistling, he soon realized was voices—*singing*? The cave widened and they found themselves pushing aside long white drapes that served as a sort of door. Stepping out of the cave into a huge courtyard flooded with light from the rising sun, Lam was sure he had entered an imaginary world. The courtyard was filled with singing people, their backs to the newcomers. They were dressed in simple tunics of various colors.

Leading the singing was a man who stood on some steps and faced the others, his hands lifted high. He did not notice Lam and Padu at first, but Lam saw that the leader had the same height and complexion as Padu.

The sunshine splashed through a transparent dome which spanned not only the courtyard, but fields of grain, gardens with splashing fountains, and a dozen buildings. *Was that a stream running through the gardens?* Lam wondered, trying to bring reality to this apparent illusion. The surface of the water was glittering in the morning light. Lam surveyed the sight in awe. He had seen larger domes before, but never one so beautiful. And everything seemed to be in harmony, even the singing.

Now the voices began to quiet as one person after another turned to view the two new arrivals. Lam instantly felt like a zoo creature as thirty pairs of eyes thoroughly examined him and his pilgrim-rescuer. Then he noticed that the amulet Padu wore around his neck glowed brightly and illumined his still-hooded face. Padu drew his hood back and looked straight at the one on the steps. The man's mouth opened in surprise; he fell to his knees and cried in a dialect unfamiliar to Lam,

"Ma Arna!" Then in Common, "Your Highness!"

Chapter Two

Spending the next day nursing his sore hand and resting, Lam could think more clearly. He still did not understand what was going on here, but he determined to get out as soon as possible. Although the colony was a lovely place, the people here were peculiar—their quietness and calm was like nothing he had ever sensed. His restless spirit felt compressed by their restraint. Lam sat on a stone bench in the flower garden as the setting sun seemed to ignite the foliage with golden flames. But even the beauty of the place did not diminish his conviction: He had to get out of here. Yet, he began to feel even more that leaving was not his choice to make.

"So, Padu, you are finally going to return to Tsu. I must go with you," said Maxai, the man in charge of the group singing when the strangers arrived.

"What about your responsibilities here?" asked the King.

"We have developed strong leaders who are running the colony. Perhaps it is time they were on their own. If you asked them, they might tell you I'm already not needed here."

Padu pulled thoughtfully on his chin.

"Be reasonable, Padu!" pleaded Maxai. "You plan to return to Tsu, but you don't even know how; you plan to rally those loyal to the Way of Tsu, but you don't know what to expect. Then, you plan to defeat the occupying forces? Are you also planning to fight alone? We have received no news of Tsu for some time now. Your Highness, even a king needs a little help now and then."

Padu chuckled and said, "My friend, you are again right—

and persuasive. How can I resist such an offer? Now I see why you were sent as an ambassador. I gladly welcome your company and your assistance."

Maxai grinned and shook the King's hand. He was delighted to serve the King and eager to return to his home planet, Tsu, even if circumstances there were dangerous. He was no stranger to peril. The trouble there only strengthened his desire to return and help the King. He loved to be on the front lines, which was why, so many years ago, he had asked the Council to send him as an ambassador to Saan.

"I remember hearing of your early adventures on Saan when I first visited here," said Padu, "how you defied the priest of Ludaii and survived so many violent attacks. You made a strong community that could withstand the magic of Ludaii—and the Doomen, when they came."

Somewhere a bell rang and cut Padu short. Maxai informed the King and Lam that it was time to join the other colonists in a feast to be held in the King's honor. The meal was the first pleasure Lam could look forward to since he had entered the tavern for a quiet drink the night before.

The meal of home-grown foods was served at long tables with benches. Jubilant over the luscious feast, Lam still realized he'd better take advantage of the free-flowing conversations. With that in mind, he sat next to a young colonist and began grilling him for any information that might help him understand what he had gotten into.

"What can you tell me about Tsu?" asked Lam.

"Well, I haven't heard any recent news," began Lam's dinner companion. His Saanian accent was difficult to understand, especially above the dinner clamor, but Lam was fairly adept at foreign dialects because of his travels.

"That doesn't matter. Just tell me *anything* you know about Tsu," said Lam.

After a few long moments of thoughts and a few swallows of food, the man began. "As Padu maybe has told you, Tsu sent out ambassadors to other planets about a generation ago. Saan was one of those planets. Then, as I understand it, about fifteen years ago the Doomen invaded Tsu and killed or scattered the leadership. The King barely escaped." The man swallowed some of his drink while Lam digested what he had been told.

"The King visited Saan shortly after his escape. Some of us would not bow to the Dominion when the Doomen came to our planet. Padu strengthened us when we were ready to give up. Of course, we could not long withstand the Dominion Forces, so we built this city of refuge. The Dominion has searched the planet but have never discovered us. We trade secretly with the port town."

The man seemed proud of these accomplishments, but his countenance suddenly fell and his tone grew grave. "At that time the King stayed a while, but I sense this visit will be brief. Look at them."

It was true, thought Lam as he watched Padu urgently discussing matters with the elders of the colony, Chen and Jehd, who sat beside him. Lam could not hear the conversation, but he too sensed that it was serious—too serious. Somehow he was sure the discussions included his future. His heart began to race and the perspiration flowed.

That night Lam tossed with nightmares. Although the night was cool, he woke several times in a profuse sweat. When daylight finally came, he could not recall the dreams, but a lingering sense of foreboding chilled his heart. He sat on the edge of the bed, straining to remember what dream could possibly have given him such an uneasy feeling. The answer remained just beyond the reach of his consciousness—so close but still a universe away. When he finally pulled his lethargic body out of its slumber and had washed, a young man greeted him and led him to a private garden where the King and Maxai were having breakfast.

Lam managed a cordial nod to the other men, as he seated himself beside them.

"Good morning, Lam," said Padu with more enthusiasm than Lam had mustered. "How did you sleep?"

"I've slept better during an ion storm. Listen, Padu, I'm tired of your beating around the bush. Something's got me spooked. Give me some facts or I leave."

Maxai shot a concerned look to Padu, but Padu remained calm and his gaze assured Lam that it was "understandable."

"Maybe you understand it," returned Lam, "but all I know is that the sooner I'm on my way about my own business the better."

"Are you hungry?" asked Padu, passing Lam a platter of fruits and bread from a serving cart beside the table.

"Why do you keep changing the subject all the time?" demanded Lam, pointing his bandaged hand at Padu as if it were a weapon. "You have a way of not giving me answers."

"Actually, I've never changed the subject. You forget that you're disorientated and confused. Nevertheless, it's time to determine causes and solutions."

"What's that supposed to mean?"

Maxai jumped in. "Lam, what do you know about the Dominion—and Doomen in particular?"

Lam glanced down at his food and started pushing it around on his plate. He was looking for answers, not questions—especially *that* question.

After an uncomfortable silence, Maxai continued, "I mean, the Doomen have more power than most people realize—seemingly supernatural. You and Padu have killed one of them—"

"Listen," Lam interrupted impatiently, "I know plenty about the Dominion, and as for Doomen, it's not the first time—" Lam cut himself off, having already said more than he had intended. *If only I could think as fast as I move my mouth*, he groaned inwardly.

Maxai looked over at Padu to observe his reaction to Lam's words. The King was scrutinizing Lam as if to peer inside him. Maxai decided to finish his story.

"Lam, don't you realize that you are an accomplice of one of the Dominion's greatest enemies? You escaped from a carefully planned ambush. The reason Padu led you through the back alleys is that seventy-five Doomen soldiers were combing the port city in order to trap and kill him."

"Seventy-five?" gasped Lam. "How could we possibly have gotten away?"

"The Dominion is not the only power in the universe," answered Padu.

Lam was incredulous. Were they telling the truth about the

Doomen? He had never heard of anyone escaping such a trap. Padu and his friends were hiding something, something big— he was sure of it. What could it be?

"Why should the Dominion care about a crazy pilgrim like you? Or any of you here? What are you people trying to hide?" Lam rose to his feet as he demanded answers.

"You still are not ready to know," answered Padu evenly.

Lam pushed his hand through his hair, took a deep, angry breath and walked to the garden wall. He leaned against it, his back to Padu and Maxai. *One more look at that calm face and I'll explode*, Lam thought.

Maxai spoke first. "Some of our colony have sensed the searching of the Doomen minds. We believe they are searching for the King *and* for you."

"We must leave here, friend," said Padu to Lam. "Our presence endangers the lives of everyone in the colony, and you are aware of what the Doomens' would do, aren't you?"

"You're finally seeing things my way," said Lam. "I think."

"Well, not quite," said Padu slowly. "I need your help."

"That figures," grunted Lam after returning to the table and swallowing some breakfast. "I knew there had to be something in it for you. I suppose you want a ride out of here." Lam purposely limited his offer, but one glance at the solemn appearance of the King's face said they wanted more than a ride.

"Lam," began Padu quietly, "I intend to return to Tsu as king and free our people from the tyranny of the Doomen."

"Uh-huh . . ." Lam's face flushed and his eyes dropped as he began pushing food around on his plate. "Are you insane?" he inquired quietly. "Don't you remember Entar?" The King nodded but said nothing. Lam took a deep breath and seemed to collect himself. "And I suppose you want me to be your general or something."

Padu managed a laugh and said, "Or something." Then he grew solemn again, "Having a license for trading, you can penetrate virtually any defense without raising suspicion. And your cargo holds can be modified to carry weapons. We have discussed the plan thoroughly and feel you are our best opportunity—perhaps our only opportunity. Maxai and I intend to impersonate your assistants."

Lam pushed back his chair as he searched the face of the King. *These guys are as serious as they are crazy*, he thought. "There's no way we could work it," was the best reply he could manage.

Maxai's face flushed with concern, but Padu simply asked, "If you don't go with us, where will you go?"

Padu's words pierced Lam like a lighttorch. Lam was overwhelmed by the feeling that Padu knew much more about him than had been revealed. *Where is he getting his information anyway?* As Lam weighed his options, he concluded that this was one of those times when he needed to compromise.

Lam slid his chair forward to make one last attempt to get out of this trouble. "I'm not who you think I am. Your lives are endangered if you include me."

Padu returned, "Lam, do you honestly think I am interested in safety?"

Lam put his elbow on the table and rested his head in his hand. After a few long moments he looked up and sighed, "We'll all probably regret this—"

Padu gave him no chance to finish his sentence and said, "We must prepare to leave immediately."

"Can't I at least finish my breakfast?" protested Lam. He stuffed his food down as quickly as possible, then found Padu already sending out parties to equip the snow-covered ship. By midafternoon, Lam, Padu, Maxai and most of the people from the colony were gathered in the main courtyard. Lam noticed again that the stone in the King's amulet was glowing intensely; this time he also noticed that nearly everyone wore a ring or amulet with that same kind of glowing stone. Noticing that fewer people were gathered now than before, Lam asked a woman nearby where the others were.

"Many of our people are gathered to resist the Doomen's power. They must not be allowed to discover our colony—or you and the King."

"Are they going to shoot it out?" asked Lam, fingering the pistol beneath his tunic.

The woman smiled. "There are other ways."

Other ways? Lam felt like a character in a ghost story—getting information out of these people was like pulling teeth. They seemed so content to live in this fantasy land. He thought to rephrase his question to the woman, but Maxai walked up the steps to address the company.

"Friends and loved ones, several years ago King Padeus realized he must return to Tsu to expel the Doomen. Tsu must regain her place in the galaxy as the cradle of freedom. As you know, this colony has determined that I should accompany King Padeus and our new friend, Lam Laeo, on this mission. The enormity of this venture is beyond anything ever attempted. To my knowledge, no planet has ever resisted the Dominion and survived. . . ."

The group stood quietly after Maxai spoke. Lam surveyed the assembled group. No one appeared impassioned; most appeared concerned; and a few seemed shaken and near tears.

The trembling of the woman next to Lam startled him. "I must express what I feel," she called out. "These men will be equal to the peril they will face—but we will not see the King again on This Side."

The silence of a grave followed and a mortal horror ran through Lam. Though he had never trusted such apparently superstitious feelings, the woman's words somehow imbued his skeptical mind. *She must be a lunatic*, he hoped.

"Forgive me please, but I must speak the truth," the woman continued, pointing to the King. "This man will be captured if he goes to Tsu, and *he will be killed*."

Chapter Three

In near darkness Kurdon kneeled before the massive stone altar. His powerful body looked as though it had been chiseled from the same stone. Crimson flames from torches flanking the altar dimly revealed hideous carvings in the altar's black stone. A monstrous serpent with powerful wings and talons twisted in one part tyrannized the central carving. Beneath its atrocious form a strange procession of smaller creatures was pictured as carrying dead bodies to the serpent. Nearby were carved scenes of torture and torment, some of them lewd and sadistic. The flames played on the scenes, making their figures to move with the shifting shadows: The serpent's wings appeared to fold and unfold, and its glowing red eyes gazed on the silent worshiper below.

Halfway down the hall, two paneled doors opened to other parts of the immense palace. Just inside those doors a thin, elderly man with a strangely puckered face waited fretfully with urgent news for his master. But having been Kurdon's personal attendant for years, he knew better than to disturb his master while he kneeled.

As Kurdon slowly rose from his knees, the light from the torches grew dimmer, while the light from several elaborate crystal chandeliers in the hall grew brighter, as if to signify he had finished drawing power from the altar. His handsome but sharply chiseled features kept their intensity as he opened his eyes and rose to his feet. His tunic and trousers were simple, but over his shoulders he wore a white woven cape with gold trim and a high collar. A serpent like the one carved on the altar was sewn in gold on the back of his cape. On his massive chest he wore a breastplate with a deeply etched star-shaped design, and at each point of the star lay a scarlet-colored stone, similar to the glowing stones in the serpent's eyes on the altar.

"Speak," ordered Kurdon as he neared the pucker-faced man at the doors. His voice sounded menacing despite his face remaining unnaturally calm. His command still echoed in the lifeless hall when his servant responded.

"Exalted Kurdon," began Scurvit, his head bowed low, "the capture force has returned from Saan. Although they seized his ship, Padeus has escaped. The Doomen commander reports only occasional success in sensing his presence. Something still works against them, so he says. But they were able to definitely confirm that Padeus left the planet."

Kurdon stood expressionless for a moment and then swept through the doors into the lighted and lavishly decorated palace halls. As Scurvit rushed to keep up, other servants and assistants swarmed like bees around Kurdon. A few, like Scurvit, served Kurdon for gain, but most had been conscripted from conquered planets and served him from abject fear.

"Scurvit, bring the Doomen commander to my chamber," Kurdon charged as they walked. To a uniformed man he called sharply, "Ready three Doomen fighters and my flagship. I will go to Saan myself and discover why the Doomen were thwarted. This 'king' will soon learn of the power with which he toys."

Scurvit puffed as he walked down the long halls as quickly as his old body could go. He bent over a little more than usual as he leaned into this task, and he folded his hands in front of him trying to keep his many rings from falling off in his haste. The exertion made him warm, a sensation seldom enjoyed; he was usually bone-chilled in the stone and glass palace. A death-like chill seemed to possess the colossal structure.

Scurvit finally reached the rotunda and stepped into the lift. With a heave he managed to shut the wrought metal gate over the cage door.

"To the port," Scurvit said into the control panel. The cage suddenly hurled upward, causing Scurvit to grab his abdomen. "I'll never get used to this thing," he sputtered.

For fear of becoming dizzier, Scurvit did not dare nor care to take in the spectacular view of the palace rotunda. Colored skylights in the dome illuminated exquisite paintings and ornate carvings plundered from many planets in the Dominion. Polished stone columns and arches provided structural support. And from his height, if he had been looking, Scurvit could have clearly seen the grand mosaic on the rotunda's floor: a twisting, winged serpent—the Dominion's ominous emblem.

Scurvit finally reached the port. It stood atop the west wing of the palace and was reserved for the palace guard, the Doomen commander's ship and Kurdon's matchless flagship. He passed through the rest area where a few crew members were totally absorbed in a childish stick game. A young, low-ranking officer named Kalen quickly straightened up and saluted when he noticed Scurvit. The other crew members reluctantly followed his example. Scurvit hastily returned the gesture and then pushed through the glass doors into the hangar. He found the ever-vigilant Doomen commander standing by his ship.

"The Exalted Kurdon wishes to see you in his chambers," bellowed Scurvit above the maintenance crews' hammering and his own echo. "I will escort you personally." Scurvit waited for the Doomen to move or acknowledge him, but he only continued the silent vigil. Finally Scurvit decided just to start walking. Glancing over his shoulder, he saw that the Doomen followed.

Kurdon and the Doomen commander faced each other across a table in Kurdon's chamber. Had anyone else failed in such a mission, he would have been killed without questioning, but Kurdon was not angry at the Doomen—it would have been pointless. Doomen were far too valuable. Their minds could probe another's and reveal fear—or instill it. They were strong, tireless, heartless and obedient.

"Padeus was trapped," explained the Doomen in his usual grating voice and with few words. "We guarded corners and searched buildings. One of us was destroyed in a tavern confrontation. We tracked Padeus and another unknown through the city, but he had hidden a second ship. When last we met minds, he was fleeing the planet."

"Before Saan, Padeus was in the Ante Demarian system. Have your patrols found anything there?" asked Kurdon, leaning closer to the Doomen.

"They know he was on planet Seven," the Doomen rasped. "They search now."

Outside Kurdon's chamber, Scurvit and a young aide waited for further orders.

"I have never seen him like this," whispered the aide in a toneless voice. The puckered old man surveyed both halls to make sure no one was listening, and then took the opportunity to show just how much he knew. He loved to impress the young aides.

"Our master never acts on impulse," Scurvit explained in hushed tones. "And of course he never acts out of anger—he is beyond mere emotion. But every attempt to capture King Padeus has failed, and it is beginning to impact him. He now believes the failure is a reflection on his leadership. Our master will triumph, but it is leaving his fists clenched a little tighter than usual."

"How can one man be such a threat, um—I mean a problem to the Dominion?"

"You are probably too young to remember the days when the Dominion began. The planets fought among themselves and the Interplanetary Alliance Police Force was so unmanned and powerless that space piracy was rampant. Our master, through the Doomen, offered each planet peace and protection—at a price of course. Entar refused our help and we made it a prime example of what happens to resisting planets. Most were happy to accept our help after that.

"But there was and is a queer sect called 'The Way of Tsu.' Its followers usually refuse allegiance to the Dominion, and many travel about the galaxy stirring up discontent. Our master has had to deal harshly, for their own good, with several planets infected by this insubordinate sect. King Padeus is the former ruler of Tsu, and he continues to elude capture and cause malcontent. The Doomen recently tracked him all the way from the Ante Demarian system to Saan, surrounded the port city and he still gave them the slip. Some suggest they still have *power*!"

Kurdon's door slid open and Scurvit snapped to attention. The displeasure written in the lines of his face said they were bound for the planet Saan.

Chapter Four

They'll be guarding the light gate," said Lam to his passengers, Padu and Maxai. "What's the plan?" Starjumper had left its snowy pad in Saan's mountains without incident, and the Tsuian colony was appearing smaller by the moment through the viewing port.

"I have heard," replied Padu, choosing his words carefully, "that there are unguarded light gates—gates that the Dominion does not know about. . . ."

Lam turned from his viewing screen to meet Padu's gaze. The King's dark, Tsuian eyes seemed to see more than Lam cared to disclose. *How can he know so much?* wondered Lam as he glanced nervously back at his instruments.

"You're right," said Lam brusquely. "There are light gates hidden from the Dominion. We could use one I know about on the dark side of Scallon's moon—Scallon is the fourth planet from Saan's sun." Lam shot a quick glance at Padu and then Maxai. "Just don't ask me any more about it, okay?" Lam added, almost irately.

"Certainly," agreed Maxai, sounding a bit confused. Padu said nothing and simply turned and gazed out the viewing port.

After an uncomfortably long silence, Padu said to his companions, "I am sorry I did not tell you where we are bound, but the Doomen were trying to meet minds. The risks that they might discover something of our plans were very high. We are safely out of their mind-range now."

"I hope we find out eventually so I can point this ship in the right direction," mumbled Lam.

"Are you afraid we will wander in space as we did the back alleys of Saan?" laughed Padu. "By the way, did you ever clean your slimy clothes? They may have disintegrated by now. Well, so much for the past. Lam, our destination is the seventh planet of the Ante Demarian system."

"I didn't know there were any habitable planets there," said Lam, immersed in thought.

"You're right, but we're not going for a friendly visit. There is something there we want," responded Padu, a hint of sadness in his voice. Lam waited for more information, but none came. His tolerance of the secrecy game had just about come to an end. There was nothing *he* wanted there, that was for sure.

Lam busied himself checking instruments and entering the coordinates for the light gate of the Ante Demarian system and for the secret light gate in Saan's system. Once entered, he left his seat and returned a few moments later with a fresh wrap for his hand. The swelling had gone down and he hoped he could wrap it with less material. He had a feeling he might need its use again soon.

As he wrapped, Lam asked, "We are posing as traders in Monobarite stones?" Maxai, who was seated behind Lam and Padu, leaned forward and nodded yes. Lam continued, "And Monobarite is the substance you and the colonists wear in rings and amulets?"

"We call them M-stones," said Maxai, "and they are rare— only a few planets have significant deposits. Few people know enough about Monobarite for it to become a medium of exchange as are other gems."

"These have at least one exceptional quality," said Lam, looking at the gently glowing stone in Padu's amulet.

"Yes," continued Maxai. "They give off light when in proximity to other M-stones. No one knows why. The more there are together, the brighter they get."

Maxai took the pouch that hung from his belt and opened it in front of Lam. A light as brilliant as the brightest sun bathed their faces, and rays danced out of the pouch as Maxai tilted the bag back and forth.

"Tsu has M-stone deposits," continued Maxai. "When we started sending ambassadors, we sent these stones with them. That way, as they traveled, they could easily recognize other

Tsuians by their glowing stones."

"Fascinating," said Lam as Maxai put the stones away. That explained why he was not given the stones even though he was supposed to be a dealer in them. Still, the stones could be profitable after this unpleasant experience was over. He knew of other materials that emitted light, but that was usually due to a breakdown in their atomic structure. Other stones, such as Redlyn, emitted no energy of their own, but amplified light energy from other sources and made it efficient for weapons.

"Does Monobarite have any practical use, like Redlyn?" probed Lam.

"Not that I know of," answered Maxai. Padu continued in sober thought, saying nothing. Lam wondered what he might know and wasn't telling.

After a few moments of such musing, Lam returned his thought to the instruments. "We are approaching the light gate," he announced.

"I've heard there's a new Emec that de-masses with less waste," said Maxai to Lam. Seeing that Lam loved his ship and wanted to talk, he thought it would be good for conversation.

"It's been around for years," said Lam, "but I haven't seen it. Starjumper's Emec is extremely efficient anyway. When we re-mass at the destination gate, we'll have only lost Redlyn the size of my hand."

The viewing screen placed a grid pattern over the stars and concentric squares over the grid so it appeared as if they were flying down a rectangular tunnel. The smallest center square was flashing, and as they flew closer to the light gate, the square grew larger.

"Strap in and get comfortable," advised Lam. "We'll be passing the light gate in a few seconds."

The moment the flashing square filled the screen Starjumper passed three satellites that formed the unusually small light gate. Lam examined the indicators for the Emec. They showed that the ship was already starting to convert to energy and the Emec was coding properly so that the energy could be converted back to mass at the destination gate.

The ship began to shimmer and lose definition. Inside, the

passengers felt the tingling and saw the shimmering. Warning buzzers rang but the men no longer comprehended sound. With a brilliant flash Starjumper disappeared like an ener-bolt as it ripped through space toward the destination gate in the Ante Demarian system.

On the barren planet Seven, two surveillant Doomen kicked up rust-colored dust as they walked toward a large rock formation. The stones had the appearance of elderly giants hunched together and squatting in the colorful earth. It was the fifth such out-cropping they had inspected on the planet, having yet to turn up a clue. But as they neared it, they could see that the rocks concealed the indistinct outline of the mouth of a cave. They stopped to withdraw their pistols and then proceeded cautiously to the obscure cave.

Chapter Five

The tavern-keeper stood frozen in unimaginable horror as the heavy door was blasted to slivers and the intruders stormed in. Towering over him was the unmistakable frame of Kurdon, who was flanked by six Doomen with pistols raised. The pulsating red glow from the stones in Kurdon's breastplate illuminated their desolate faces. The tavern-keeper wished by Ludaii he had let them in when they knocked instead of saying, "Go away, we're closed."

"You had visitors here that killed one of my soldiers," Kurdon began coldly. "I understand you talked with one and saw the other. Who were they?"

The stunned tavern-keeper's heart was in his mouth as he searched for words to answer.

"He—one was an older man, with a hood." He paused to see if Kurdon was accepting the information.

"Go on," ordered Kurdon.

"The other was a younger man—a merchant, I think."

"Do you know this merchant's name?" asked Kurdon.

"No. I'd never seen him in here before."

"Did he have an accent? Do you know where he came from?"

"I barely spoke with him," the tavern-keeper faltered, hoping to be let off the hook. Kurdon's sinister eyes threatened his extinction as he wiped his sweaty palms on his apron. "But it sounded like he was an Entarian, but—but that's impossible. The Dominion, that is, Entar was destroyed."

"What did he look like?"

The tavern-keeper broke into a cold sweat. He knew he did not have the information his visitors were after, and he was aware of Kurdon's lack of mercy. "It was dark, and I didn't really . . ."

Kurdon signaled the nearest Doomen who stepped forward and grazed the tavern-keeper on the side of the head with the butt of his pistol. The man collapsed behind the bar, holding his head. Kurdon stepped behind the bar and pressed his boot down on the man's bloodied head.

"Try to remember."

"Like I said," the tavern-keeper gasped between moans, "he was young, maybe thirty. He was not really heavy or thin. He had sandy hair, not long. He had a concealed pistol that the soldier disarmed him of. I can't remember any more—really I can't. Please let me go, please!"

"How did they leave?" Kurdon uttered, pressing harder.

"Through the back door."

Kurdon turned and headed out the front door frame, followed by his Doomen contingent. Scurvit was waiting outside the door, wondering if they had been successful. Noticing Kurdon's tightly clenched fist convinced him it was better to say nothing. Climbing into their transport skips, they sped back to the port where the ships waited.

Kurdon's flagship and the Doomen fighters were designed to instill fear. Kurdon's ship was black and highly polished. Flanking the hull were angled panels that connected at the top and acted as landing stabilizers, solar energy collectors and weapon mounts. From the front it looked like a deadly insect. The Doomen fighters flanked the flagship. They, too, were highly polished black, but they were larger and more functional, not as sleek. Their six legs that extended for landing gave the fighters the same giant insect-like appearance as Kurdon's flagship. Two large semi-spherical viewing ports served as "eyes." Each ship, including the transport skips, was emblazoned with a twisting serpent like that carved into Kurdon's altar.

Kurdon himself was a totally intimidating figure, but one would be hard-pressed to say why. He was actually good-looking; he was tall and muscular, his features rugged. His light hair and eyes contrasted with his olive complexion. His clothes were simple white and gold. Yet everyone who met him trembled.

Paralyzing dread accompanied his presence.

When the skips reached the port, one of the Doomen stationed on Saan met his master.

"We sense a corporate presence," rasped the Doomen as Kurdon stepped from the skip. "Our scouts return," it added, gesturing skyward where the shadow of a Doomen fighter appeared, growing quickly larger as it approached, until only a moment later it hovered above them. Turning his face toward the hovering craft, the Doomen again looked at Kurdon. "In the central mountains of this continent."

Kurdon knew what the Doomen sensed. "The Way of Tsu," he breathed in a hushed tone. "That explains much. Your scouts will lead us there now."

For days the Doomen mind-invasion had assaulted the mountain colony. The colonists did all they could to remain calm, but had never been so heavily attacked. The gray-haired Chen was now the appointed leader and was discussing the warfare with his younger friend Jehd.

"I don't know what to do," Chen said, appealing for help. "When Padu left, all of their power focused on us. Should we implement plans to evacuate? Or should we gather the few weapons we have and take a stand?" Chen's resistance was nearly worn out.

"We must decide something soon," noted Jehd. "Every time a Doomen touches one of our minds, we fear more; and it opens the door for them to meet our minds again. It is an alarming experience. Touching their minds is like touching a dead animal crawling with parasites—it's defiling."

Saying this, Jehd stopped disquietingly. His face grew ashen and his eyes glazed. Chen knew that his friend was meeting a Doomen, but he did not seem to be trying to block it out. Jehd fell to his knees, then appeared to finally resist. Taking his hand, Chen helped him up.

"They are closer than they have been all day. And they are coming closer."

"I hoped it would never come to this," stated Chen, assured that his short-term leadership had doomed them all.

"It's so much stronger than before, though, Chen. There must be more Doomen; perhaps a mobilized strike force. The presence is more, well, more ominous."

Chen stared at the stones in the walkway for a moment of intense reflection. He knew what must be done. He turned and strode quickly to the plaza. Jehd followed. Chen rang a bell which was used to gather the people. In moments the plaza was filled. Some expressed fear; some, sadness; some, anger; some, confusion; others, calm. Many of the children were crying. Chen stood on the steps to address the assembly.

"Friends, for several days we have lived in perpetual fear because of our enemies," Chen began. "We have planned and prayed, wept and waited. As many of you now sense, the waiting is nearing an end. But we must recall that when we vowed to follow the Way of Tsu, we did so with no guarantee of safety or comfort. Our time on This Side may be short, but we need not fear. If it comes to that, let us remember the joy awaiting us on the Other Side."

In the sky above, Kurdon rose from his seat, having spotted the glint of the colony's dome in his viewing screen. Pressing a button on the arm of his seat, he dispassionately gave orders to the pilots of the fighters which flanked his flagship.

"When in range, fire on the dome. We will land in the city."

The dark ships were like holes in the blue sky—a sky suddenly torn by the red bolts which leaped from the outer ships and struck the dome with a thunderous crash. The redness spread from the point of impact as if it were a many-armed beast engulfing its prey. In a second a large section of the dome was gone—melted, collapsed or ripped off in the initial explosion. Kurdon's ships descended unchallenged through the hole and landed upon the smoldering rubble. Doomen from each ship poured out, running with shoulder-blasters in front of them. Forming an armed corridor, they stood at attention for their master's arrival.

Kurdon swept down from his ship, his cape unfurling behind him, animating the serpent emblazoned on it. When he reached the middle of the column, the Doomen guards that flanked him started marching. The portentous procession headed for the center of the plaza. Kurdon signaled the Doomen commander who ordered a halt, and the company stood facing the steps where the colonists had met moments before.

"Interrogate everyone you find in this city. Use any method needed. Then kill them," ordered Kurdon coolly. The Doomen soldiers, weapons readied, fanned out to search the city. Entering a house alone, a Doomen threw open doors and turned over furniture. He pounded on the walls for hollow spots. Behind a cabinet in the room, a family hid in a secret hollow. They held their breaths and hoped the Doomen would not hear the pounding of their hearts or sense their panic-stricken minds. Then their baby girl began to cry. The trembling mother had tried to comfort her, but too late.

The Doomen stopped and turned toward the cabinet. He flung aside the cabinet, which crashed to the floor, shattering the dishes and other valuables it held. The Doomen stepped near the hollow in the wall. The Way of Tsu had protected them before, but now the terror of the Dominion loomed above them. The Doomen surveyed the hole but looked past them, seemingly blind to their presence. The Doomen's shadowed areas that served as eyes behind his padded helmet strained to search the hiding spot as one grasping at fleeting shadows or trying to identify a distant sound. He turned his head from one corner to the other. The mother clutched her daughter tightly and stroked her hair to keep her quiet. The Doomen held out its hand as if trying to feel their presence. After what seemed an ill-fated eternity, the Doomen simply turned and left the house.

Each returning Doomen reported finding nothing—not one person.

"You sense no presence?" Kurdon asked the Doomen commander. They did not.

"Perhaps they have all killed themselves. I smell something that sickens me; perhaps it is their rotting flesh."

"Shall we destroy the city?" asked the Doomen commander.

Kurdon stood gazing over the city. The cool mountain wind moaned through the gash in the dome as if the wind felt the pain.

Kurdon finally replied curtly, "More urgent matters await elsewhere. Now that we have uncovered this rebel nest, no one will ever come here." The place unsettled him.

The troops followed their master to the ships, their boots grinding fragments of broken dome as they marched. Soon the city was again quiet except for the moaning wind. It did not stay quiet long though. Kurdon missed quite a celebration that night.

A re-massing ship, shimmering and ghost-like, appeared in the light gate that served the sparse Ante Demarian system. Lam rubbed his eyes and shook his hands to restore feeling. He quickly checked the instruments to make sure they were properly programmed to direct the ship to Planet Seven, then leaned back in his seat, folded his arms, and studied the face of the older pilgrim.

"When that woman said you'd be killed on Tsu," Lam began, "you appeared to believe her."

"I did," replied Padu staidly. "She spoke by the Power."

"I don't understand. Is this Power some sort of religion?"

Maxai looked knowingly at Padu, who finally was deciding to give Lam a fuller explanation.

Padu began, "You perhaps have heard about the Way of Tsu—"

"I heard some of your colonist friends mention it."

"I will not bother you with many details, but there are some facts you should know: Tsu is the birthplace of the Cathra, the Hidden Way, commonly known as the Way of Tsu. We serve only the Source and the Power."

"The Source and the Power are gods?" asked Lam.

"He is God," said Maxai.

Lam leaned forward and tapped the instrument panel in thought. "Well, I've been halfway around the civilized galaxy. I've seen many things, but no gods—at least not any that mattered much."

"You say you've been halfway around the galaxy?" Padu queried.

"Sure."

"Then you've seen a small portion of His handiwork."

Chapter Six

How are things going up there?" Wil, a tall young man in soiled clothes, shouted up to a pair of feet protruding from an opening in the ship—one of many ships in the vaulted subterranean hangar. The first answer to Wil's question was muffled, but after considerable effort, the owner of the feet appeared—a lovely young woman with an olive complexion and long black hair that strayed wispily from beneath her work cap. Such delicate beauty was accented by the contrast of her grim surroundings.

"Fine," she answered, wiping her blackened hands on a rag, "except I still can't get those panels to line up. Got any bright ideas?"

"Not now, Melena," Wil called. "The Council meets in fifteen minutes, and I thought you might like to wash your face." Melena hurled the rag at him, but he successfully dodged it. He walked away with a smirk and congratulated himself that he had out-thought his sister once again. Most of the time he beat her to the throw.

When Melena joined the others in the Council chambers, she looked more like a high-ranking official than a fighter mechanic. Her gown was laced with gold and silver thread and she wore a pendant with a white, softly glowing stone. The padded soles of her slippers made no sound on the wooden floor. She gently pushed aside the colored banners hanging from the walls as she made her way past groups of robed men and women already engaged in heated discussions. She took her place next to Wil at the arc-shaped table and listened as her uncle motioned for quiet. An intense silence fell as he began to relate the grievous news.

39

"The situation is as we had feared," announced Hud, his face uncharacteristically creased by a frown. "I met with Governor Cathra early this morning. You all know that he and I once served together on the royal Council of Tsu. Today he treated me as a rebel and a traitor. He forced me to meet with him in the old Council chamber—with him seated in the *King's* seat flanked by guards."

An angry murmur rose from the group.

Hud continued, "His increasing authority seems to have blinded him to the fact that we are occupied by the Dominion—we did not invite the Doomen to our planet."

"And many lives have already been lost because of it!" interjected Wil.

"Indeed," Hud added sadly. "We recognize the sinister nature of our captors. Since the Doomen came, death rules Tsu. We must take action against them, but what action is best?"

Melena listened attentively as the Council reviewed and examined the newest information and considered their various courses of action. She was unsure about what to do next or what to think about Governor Cathra. It appeared that no one else did either.

After the meeting ended, solemn-faced Council members quietly drifted from the chambers still confused and without clear direction. Melena returned to her room, which, like the hangar, was carved from stone. Lying down on her bed, it felt good to release her worries and simply stare at the ceiling. Small M-stones, clustered together and embedded in the stone ceiling, provided a soft, white light. The shutters over the M-stones were half closed, but she could still see some of the stones' steady glow.

"How I wish the Power would provide us with light as steady," she whispered to herself. Then she closed her eyes and her soul sighed a prayer. Things were finally happening after fifteen years, but not the way the people had hoped. All signs so far indicated they were going from bad to desperate.

A low tone from her com-screen disturbed her rest. She rolled onto her side and saw the face of her uncle appear on the screen. "Are you there, Melena?"

Melena rose and pressed a bar under the screen and answered, "Yes."

"Would you meet me in the garden, my dear?"

"Certainly. I'll be there in a moment." She went to her wardrobe and picked out a jacket.

Melena slipped the jacket over her Council gown, then left her room. She walked down the hall past the meeting rooms, the food center, worship hall, and the closed doors of sleeping quarters. She thought of all the work that had gone into making the place liveable. Many of these rooms were carved into the mountain's stone. Other areas, such as the worship hall, were dug from sand and looser rock. These rooms were larger and had metal and wooden supports. They also had finished walls, floors and ceilings. As damp drafts whistled past her, she was glad she wore a jacket.

Soon Melena entered the large cavern that served as the hangar. She followed the lighted walkway along the wall. To her right stood the fighters she had been working on earlier that day. They looked homemade but were aerodynamic enough to skip through the atmosphere, powerful enough to escape Tsu's gravity and fast enough to outrun a Doomen fighter. They were not encumbered with gravity resistors, so, while not as versatile or well-armed as Doomen fighters, they could easily outfly them. All this was theory, of course. They had been tested on the ground but never flown. The thought of her future with these crafts made Melena walk a little faster.

She followed the corridor that led to the gardens. The raised beds and hanging hydroponics helped supply food to the fugitives defying the Dominion's forces who occupied Tsu. When she stepped into the garden, now in artificial twilight, she breathed deeply of the fresh air—one thing sorely missed in her hollowed-out stone world.

"Melena," Hud called. She turned and saw her uncle approach her, opening his arms and inviting an embrace. She gladly responded, for she deeply loved him. He had been like a father to her these last fifteen years after her own father, King Padeus, had been driven from Tsu.

"Melena," Hud sighed, "what can we possibly do? How

can we free our planet with a few hundred inexperienced soldiers and a handful of untested fighters? And our weapons! Why, the Doomen are probably armed with ener-bolt throwers. The most advanced weapons we have are explosives, Redlyn pistols and carbines—and few even of those. We don't have a chance!"

"Uncle," she scolded, grabbing his arm, "where is the faith you have taught me about?"

"Perhaps it is just my age," he said calmly, taking her hand which still clutched his arm. "I often lie awake at night listening for the call to the Other Side." He chuckled as they walked on. "But, it doesn't appear that I will so easily escape what lies ahead.

"I have been organizing, negotiating and plotting for fifteen years—ever since your father left. I am discouraged and heartbroken. The thought of what Governor Cathra has become . . ." He could not find words and only shook his head.

"To think that he is named after our faith," Melena said sadly.

"In his own way, I think he believes that cooperating with the Dominion is best for Tsu. He calls it maintaining peace."

"But how can he possibly believe that the Dominion is here for our own good, to bring peace to the galaxy?" asked Melena shaking her head.

"I have no idea, Melena," Hud reflected. "Whoever or whatever is behind the Dominion, even Cathra must realize there are no real benevolent motives. But Cathra has a bit of the 'old' in him—he loves peace as we all do. But loving peace does not necessarily bring peace. Because we all love peace, it has taken fifteen years to recruit our two hundred soldiers.

"He also has a bit of the 'new' in him—selfishness, fear, greed—none of which existed in Tsu before." The last sentence was filled with increasing emotion; he released it with a sigh.

"Anyway," Hud continued after walking in silence for a while, "I guess I am most disheartened that now, not only are we preparing to fight the Doomen, but our own people oppose us. I would not hesitate to kill a Doomen—I am not sure they are even alive, but will it come down to killing our own people? It seems all the years of work, prayer, preparation and recruitment are slipping away. How can we rid the body of infection if the body embraces the disease?"

"Uncle," pleaded Melena, "you must not give up. None of us alone are bold enough or wise enough to withstand the Dominion. You have brought us together into a cohesive force; you encouraged and emboldened us for this cause. You *are* the leader and we need your strength *now*. Remember you said that our fight is not with what we can see, but with those things we cannot see. That our unseen champion, the Power, is always with us? We have hope—hope that we can win, but that is all we have now, and without you I am not sure we can even hang on to that." Melena gave way to tears as she poured out her heart. Hud pulled her close and comforted her.

"You know, dear," he said lovingly, "you have more courage than you know. That's why I asked you to meet me here; I knew you would set me straight. I don't think I am as hopeless as I may sound; I just needed to talk."

The two embraced again and then walked back the way they had come. Hud had received much more encouragement from Melena's faith than she could have dreamed—strength of character he would soon need. As they emerged from the corridor into the hangar cavern, they were met by the sound of footsteps and harsh voices. One of the guards was pushing along a prisoner whose hands were fastened behind his back and whose eyes had been blindfolded.

"We found him wandering in the restricted area. He claims to be a messenger from Cathra."

"State your message," said Hud, his voice more gentle than the guard's had been.

"Are you the one they call Hud?" questioned the messenger nervously.

"Friend," answered Hud, "you came here to deliver a message, not ask questions. I would urge you to fulfill your task with haste."

"The duly appointed and most beneficent Governor Cathra," began the messenger, straightening up and sounding more sure of himself as he delivered his well-rehearsed speech, "requests the presence of all the reactionary leaders of the unlawful defiance. He seeks their understanding and help in finding solutions to the complex problems that divide the people of Tsu."

Hud sighed, then said to the guard, "Jern, feed the prisoner and give him an isolated and guarded room where he can rest."

After the guard and his prisoner left, Hud stood with deepened furrows in his brow. Melena looked with concern at her silent, gray-haired uncle. Fifteen years of sacrifice was about to lead them to victory, or it would destroy them all.

Chapter Seven

It looks like a barren wasteland even from up here," said Lam. "Definitely a type-one planet—a lifeless rock. You fellows planning on calling this home?" They were orbiting Ante Demarian Seven, the planet where Padu had said "something" was stored.

"The locator you left is still transmitting a strong signal," said Lam to Padu. "In fact, it looks like it's right about there," he added, pointing to a flashing green dot on the screen. "You'd better strap in for our descent."

Indicator lights flashed that the cooling equipment, gravity resistors, and other landing systems were obeying their automated orders. Starjumper landed softly in a natural flat area, much preferable to their last site. Her four stout legs touched the ground and the pads sank part way in the soft red dust. The large, sleek ship, reflecting the red sun on its gleaming white hull, provided a sharp contrast to the low, jagged rocks of the planet.

"I'm sure your indicators have shown," said Padu, "the atmosphere is quite unbreathable."

"I don't think anyone will overhear you if you tell us why we're here now," said Lam, swiveling in his chair. "I'm not suiting up until you get specific."

After a moment of silence Padu began, "I haven't been sure how the Source will work. I had hoped for direction to be revealed while traveling here, but none came. I trust that the Source will not be using what is stored here. As you know, there have been many unsuccessful attempts to stop the Dominion. I have collected the leftover weapons used in several of them. Others have given me weapons as their 'safe' way of fighting the Dominion."

Lam was not surprised, although he thought Padu expected him to be. "How did you get them here?"

"Well, I've not always begged for my rides," Padu grinned. "I had a ship that was taken from me on Saan while I was in the port town."

Lam winced at the thought of ever losing Starjumper. He was surprised that Padu did not seem upset over his loss.

The trio donned environment suits that included clear helmets with com-links and stepped into the airlock. When the outside hatch opened, swirls of orange curled around them and they climbed down onto the rust-colored earth.

An uneasy feeling gripped Lam the moment he stepped out behind Maxai and Padu. Perhaps, he thought, it was the orange air, the red sun, the barren landscape, or the low gravity. Surveying the surroundings he bumped into Maxai. Padu and Maxai had stopped suddenly.

"What is it, Max?" asked Lam.

"I don't know," said Maxai. "Just a feeling, I guess." Padu nodded that he sensed it too. The group resumed their trek toward the nearby hills where the weapons were stored, raising rust-colored dust as they walked.

"I wonder," said Padu thoughtfully, "if the Doomen may have tracked me here."

"Could they have?" asked Lam.

"I don't know," answered Padu.

Moments later they reached the large rocks and stood near the wide mouth of an obscure cave.

"The weapons were hidden in here," said Padu. "They are easy to carry in this light gravity, but I installed a track along the roof of the cave to make it easier to get them out."

Lam withdrew his pistol and slipped inside the cave. Padu and Maxai waited outside.

Padu walked to a pile of stones near the cave and moved a couple of large ones. Maxai followed him. Padu reached into the pile and pulled out a Redlyn pistol. "Perhaps I'm over cautious," said Padu, "but I try to be prepared." He handed the pistol to

Maxai and then pulled another one out for himself.

"They're a bit dusty, but I think they'll work," said Padu turning his over in his hand. They were not small like the one Lam hid in his tunic, but were rather bulky, designed for use by soldiers. The two men tightened their grips on their new weapons when Lam ran from the cave and joined them.

"No need to wonder any longer about whether Doomen could track you here or not," he said breathlessly. "We'd better get behind these rocks. I hope you know how to use those things. Let's split up and surround the cave entrance."

As the men crouched into position, four Doomen soldiers emerged from the cave, pistols drawn. They were met with red bolts. Lam fired first, the high-pitched pulse of energy finding its target in the lead Doomen. The bolt ripped the Doomen open and threw him to the ground. The other Doomen swung to fire back at Lam, but two rounds from behind them destroyed one and wounded the other. The lone standing Doomen spun and fled into the cave. Lam aimed at the wounded Doomen who was reaching for his weapon—another red flash and he became a smoldering heap littering the entrance to the cave. Lam ran to the other side of the entrance where Padu and Maxai had taken their stand.

"You shoot as though you are well-practiced," said Padu, again implying that whatever Lam was hiding was not very secret. "You can now claim two Doomen to your credit. Or perhaps you would just be adding them to your score."

"Who got the other one?" asked Lam, ignoring Padu.

Maxai pointed to Padu and said, "But I managed to wound the one you finished, Lam."

Celebrating a bit early, they did not notice a thick, silvery tentacle slithering toward them through the rusty sand. It was noiseless as it crawled snakelike toward them.

"Now we must act quickly to destroy the one inside," said Padu. "We don't have much time—Doomen everywhere must know there is trouble on this planet."

Padu was not expecting Lam to answer with a scream. Glancing at Lam's left leg, they saw that the metallic tentacle had coiled itself around it and was constricting.

"Fight it, Lam!" shouted Maxai as he shot at the thing, the bolts simply scattering off the metal armor.

"It comes from the cave!" exclaimed Padu to Maxai. "And there are more coming!" Lam could only cry out and yank helplessly at the metal beast.

"How can we get inside to knock it out without getting caught ourselves?" asked Maxai. Padu immediately pointed to the ceiling of the cave.

"The track in the roof of the cave! In this low gravity, we should be able to jump high enough to grab it and pull ourselves along. We will surprise the Doomen from above."

Lam's groans urged them to the cave. Lam struggled to keep the tentacle from wrapping around his upper body and kept shooting at the approaching tentacles. Padu and Maxai tucked their guns into their boots, dodged the tentacles as they ran and jumped. Padu grabbed the track with both hands, swung his feet up and began to inch his way into the cave. Maxai caught the track with only one hand and had to swing before he caught it with the other and could follow. "Some soldier I make," he whispered to himself.

As they crept along the track, the cave floor descended, so they hung farther above the ground. It was nearly impossible in the darkness to tell just how high they were. They could, however, hear that they were getting closer to the tentacle machine. Maxai was breathing heavily from the exertion, hoping his clumsy efforts would not betray them.

Soon he heard Padu whisper through the com-link, "I see it, just ahead."

Inching closer they could see a Doomen inside the awful machine, the soldier's upper body lit by the machine's instrument panel. Meanwhile, Lam's groans and curses poured through their com-links.

"Our pistols won't knock that machine out," whispered Maxai urgently.

"We'd better drop down to the floor then and take care of that Doomen first," Padu responded energetically.

He let go of the track, fell to the cave floor, rolled, and then jumped to his feet. The Doomen jerked his head at the sound.

When Maxai tried to let go, he discovered his leg was caught in the track. The Doomen swung around in its seat and reached for his weapon. Padu unleashed a bolt at the Doomen, but it glanced off the cage surrounding the machine's seat. The Doomen returned Padu's fire, and the King jumped aside in defense.

Before Padu had a chance to shoot again, one of the machine's tentacles whipped against his chest and slammed him against one of the large guns stored in the cave. He jumped to his feet and then reached for his own gun, but the Doomen had already climbed out of the machine and had Padu clearly in his sights. Several bolts lanced the air in the cave. One hit the Doomen in the head and he fell, backward against the machine. Maxai, hanging upside down by one leg from the track, gave a victory whoop.

"Ha! I got another one!" exclaimed Maxai as he finally freed his leg and dropped to the ground where Padu sat dazed and catching his breath. Maxai ran to shut off the machine.

"So you did Max!" said Padu, using Lam's nickname for the Tsuian ambassador. "And I thank you for it. I could see the Other Side there. Now, let's go tend to our friend outside."

They found Lam leaning against the lip of the cave's mouth, holding his leg.

"I think it's broken," Lam told them.

They helped Lam back to Starjumper where Maxai tended the leg. Padu went into the cave to begin retrieving the weapons. Maxai pulled bandages tightly around Lam's leg to hold it straight on the splint. With each tug on the bandage, Lam gritted his teeth and moaned.

"Thanks for getting me out of that mess, Max," gasped Lam between Maxai's yanks.

"It seems," said Maxai, not looking up from his work, "that we owe our lives to each other—and to the Source."

Lam simply nodded and then winced again. He wasn't so sure about the Source, but now was not the time to question it.

Padu returned, dragging a large case behind him. "We must work quickly," urged Padu, walking up the ramp and joining Lam and Maxai. "More Doomen—or perhaps regular Dominion troops—will probably be here soon."

"There's a two-wheeler back there." Lam pointed to the rear of the ship. "It might make it easier to unload that cave." He then limped a few steps toward the back and pulled up some floor tiles to show Padu where they could hide some of the armaments.

"We also have large cannons and some rockets to propel the explosives," Padu said. "Those will never fit in there."

Lam whistled. "You must have been in contact with some pretty tough people."

"You know the kind that rebel," Padu said, choosing his words carefully. "Some of these weapons came from Entar." Padu looked into Lam's eyes as he said this. Lam turned away and hobbled down the ramp to one of the four large engines attached to Starjumper's sleek hull just behind her diamond-shaped wings.

He knocked on one engine shroud and said, "This one is just for show. Your cannons should fit in here."

This time it was Padu's turn to whistle.

Padu and Maxai wiped the sweat from their foreheads when they finally removed their helmets. Planet Seven rotated quickly on its axis, but the day had seemed long; and though the gravity was low, the weapons seemed to get heavier as they labored. Exhausted and half-starved, Lam handed them each a protein bar and a drink. Despite the appearance of the bar, Maxai immediately took a big bite and a long swallow. But Padu set his down and asked, "How long before we can leave?"

"As soon as you're ready," answered Lam. Unable to help much with the loading of the ship, he had spent the time readying the ship for departure.

"As soon as we wash up, we'll be ready," said Padu. Lam noticed that Padu was acting the way he had when they were being pursued on Saan: all business.

Soon they were strapped in and lifting off the planet. They could see the horizon of the planet become more curved until finally it was just an orange ball in the black of space.

"You can relax a little while," said Lam, swiveling his chair to face his passengers. We'll soon reach the light gate. I've already programmed the Emec for Tsu's light gate."

Padu did not relax as Lam suggested.

"Friends, I have an uneasy feeling," said Padu.

"It's no wonder," joked Lam. "We're sitting on enough weapons to power a quasar." Padu laughed uneasily.

Lam swung his seat back to the control panel and offered, "Maybe it would be good to scan." A small screen in front of him indicated the results of Starjumper's scan. A flashing white light showed their position. Lam cursed as a flashing red light appeared to be getting closer.

"What is it?" asked Maxai.

Lam transferred the image to the large viewing screen so they all could see.

"Doomen," said Padu, realizing the cause of his uneasiness.

Lam quickly reviewed his options. He had to tell them about his ship's guns, even though it would confirm Padu's suspicions.

"Starjumper is armed," Lam announced, "but not for defensive fighting."

Even as Lam spoke they could see through the ports that the black of space was being sliced by red bolts of energy from the Doomen fighter. Lam grabbed the manual direction controls and began swerving and rocking the ship.

"Sooner or later it's going to hit us," muttered Lam between his teeth as he leaned his body into steering. Padu and Maxai did not answer, but sat with their heads bowed. "Great," grumbled Lam. "You're some crew."

Then it came to him. "Of course!" he cried as he kicked Maxai in the shin.

"Grab some of that explosive and a detonator, arm it and put it in the garbage chutes!" Lam ordered.

Maxai leaped up and raced to the back of the ship, pulling up a loose floor tile. He prepared the explosive, shoved it in the chute and called forward to Lam. Lam had continued his evasive flying.

Lam yelled back to Maxai, "When I say so, eject it." Lam pulled Starjumper into a straight course. This maneuver seemed to surprise the Doomen fighter, which stopped shooting as it fell into a straight pursuit course. He was going to move in close for an easy shot.

"Now!" yelled Lam. Maxai leaned on the large red button and the explosives ejected. He hurried to the front in time to see a tremendous explosion on the viewing screen. A red light vanished from the scanning screen.

They all laughed in jubilation and slapped each other on the back. Padu and Maxai exclaimed repeatedly, "Thank the Source and the Power!" Lam wondered if they had forgotten it was his idea that saved them.

"Perhaps we should name our little band the 'Doomen Slayers'," joked Maxai.

"I'll be happy if we're able to call ourselves the 'Survivors'," said Lam with a dry laugh. "I'm sorry, but your relaxation time is over. We're almost to the light gate, so we'll be de-massing soon."

"Now, friends," said Padu gravely, contrasting sharply to their high spirits of seemingly moments before, "Tsu's light gate will be guarded. When we arrive you will have to present your license, Lam. Each of us must be very careful not to arouse the suspicion of the Doomen soldier. Guard your thoughts and feelings carefully."

Lam immediately told Padu of his unsuccessful attempt to shield his mind from the Doomen on Saan.

"Don't worry, Lam," Padu assured him. (It sounded like a command.) "The Power is here and will protect us."

Lam was not sure just how comforted he was by that news, but he had no time to dwell on it. The viewing screen now showed the grid pattern and the green squares of the Ante Demarian light gate.

"Strap in and get comfortable," Lam announced. "We're nearly there."

Chapter Eight

There has to be a reason for it," noted Kurdon to Scurvit. Kurdon's steely face reflected his concentration and his eyes focused beyond the walls as he paced tensely before the throne in his chamber. "The Doomen have never failed like this. Something is seriously wrong. First they lost him on Saan. Next they are victimized on Ante Demarian Seven. Then they are defeated again in space. When was the last confrontation in space?"

Scurvit was shocked that his master would so confide in him, but was immediately elated with the opportunity to offer his heady wisdom. He straightened up and prepared to take the floor.

"Well, I think—"

"I am going to the Black Hall," Kurdon interrupted. "Make sure I am not disturbed."

Scurvit sighed and nodded. Kurdon was not confiding in him, just thinking out loud. Kurdon walked to the door. It slid open and he straightened his cape collar and stepped into the hall. The door closed behind him and left Scurvit alone in his master's private chamber. He had been standing out of respect for Kurdon, but now he collapsed into one of the chairs around the conference table. It was extremely uncomfortable—designed for Doomen, he figured. Eying Kurdon's plush throne, Scurvit longed to sit there but would never dare. *Never take chances when you've got what you want*, he reasoned.

The throne, its seat black and thickly padded, was elevated two steps. Precious metals framed the throne and were magnificently shaped into the twisting serpent. Its tail descended on the left side of the throne and its front talons were curved around the right. The fierce red eyes stared over the top and scrutinized the few who desired and dared an audience with Kurdon. The serpent's wings overspread the sides of the throne, threatening to engulf those in its shadow. Scurvit lived in dread of the serpent and could never bear to look at it long.

"I certainly have less to do when he is in bowing to that thing," Scurvit noted to himself. "Yet I hate it and I hate what it does. We could get what we want without its dominance. It rules even me—I serve Kurdon, and on that account I serve this wretched beast as well."

He turned and challenged the metallic serpent, "I know the Doomen receive their breath from you—and that my master is under your direction and power. I do not know where your power comes from, but my master claims you are the Master of the Universe. I do not believe it." Scurvit stood and walked in slow defiance toward the throne. He clenched his fist daringly as if to strike it.

Scurvit gasped and pulled his hand quickly to his side as the door opened and footsteps clicked behind him. The little man whirled around to face the Doomen commander.

Scurvit caught his breath and asked, "Yes, what is your business?"

The Doomen took a few more steps, then stopped. He stood evenly facing the throne with his hands folded across his chest. No answer came. Scurvit had often nearly panicked when isolated with the Doomen. He knew the commander was constantly trying to read his mind. He fidgeted for a moment and then went back to the conference table, sat down and rested his chin in his hand. He would give the Doomen strange thoughts to read.

Soon the door opened again. Scurvit jumped to his feet and then bowed as Kurdon returned. Kurdon walked straight to his throne and sat down to face the Doomen.

"Did the Master summon you here?" required Kurdon. The Doomen nodded. "Good, that confirms my plans are correct. You reported that Padeus and his soldiers took a significant amount of weapons with them, so they must be planning to return to Tsu." He paused and thought a moment. "I will not lose that planet. If they succeed in recapturing Tsu, then other sympathetic planets will attempt the same. I will have to destroy them all as I did Entar, and wasted planets are of no use to me."

Looking squarely at the Doomen he said, "For some reason you and your Doomen have been repelled thus far. I believe it has something to do with the Tsuians' religion, but the Master pressed us to action. We cannot waste any more time with them. Prepare *all* your Doomen soldiers for immediate departure to Tsu."

Kurdon then turned to Scurvit.

"Notify the commander of the regular force to prepare all the Doomen fighters—tell him we leave for Tsu by daybreak. We will take the carrier and the destroyer along with the Doomen fighters. Order the army currently stationed here to join the other soldiers, we will leave only the palace guard and one orbiting patrol." As Scurvit bowed and nodded, Kurdon added harshly, "And warn him I will not tolerate any delays."

Day broke a frantic scene.

"Out of my way!" bellowed an officer hurrying to his shuttle. He had nearly collided with two crewmen running with a case of Redlyn rods. The officer was hoarse, and everyone was on edge. They had been up all night feverishly loading fuel and provisions, checking ships and preparing for the coming battle.

The officer's companion, a young officer himself, slapped him on the back and said, "Go easy on them—they're just doing their job."

"You're right, Kalen," admitted the officer. "But let's get to the shuttle."

Kurdon was already seated in the seat of his flagship. The seat was a smaller and less elaborate version of his throne, with communications equipment and emergency override controls built into the sides and armrest. He gazed into the viewing screen as the morning sun rose over the wall of his palace. His ship and many of the fighters were still detained in his private port.

"It is daybreak, Exalted Kurdon," said the captain of his flagship. "Shall I contact the commander and ask for a status report?"

"Affirmative," said Kurdon coldly. He knew there was a delay; otherwise the Commander General would have broadcasted flight instructions by now. Picking up the metal rod lying on his armrest, he tapped it impetuously against his hand.

56

The viewing screen in front of Kurdon spanned the entire Palace City. It sparkled in the morning sun like a pool of cool water in a desert. Kurdon's planet was a type two—it had no native life, but was not too hostile to colonize. His city had been built by the most skilled craftsmen gathered from among the conquered planets, and was lavishly adorned with the finest works of art he could find. Usually just viewing the glory of his work soothed him, but this morning even this was insufficient. He was too aware of what the delay might cost him. His communion in the Black Hall had planted in him a sense of emergency. He slapped the rod against his palm again.

An angry hand slammed against the table in the underground Council chamber. "We cannot trust the Doomen-lover!" shouted the gray-haired councilman above the loud murmur. Hud's announcement of Governor Cathra's "invitation" sparked debate all around the table.

A councilman seated near the infuriated one raised his hand, trying to calm his colleague, "But surely we must pursue a peaceful solution. This could be our last chance. Perhaps Hud's talk with Cathra has brought him to his senses."

The gray-haired one simply shook his head in disagreement and disgust. At last Hud managed to gain their attention and proceeded to deliberate on the various opinions.

"We must come to a consensus on this," began Hud. "It seems that some favor the meeting in hopes of gaining the assistance of, or at least the tolerance of, the governor. Others believe it's dangerous to attend a meeting held on his terms and conditions. As the head representation for this council, I must tell you what I think.

"The governor's message confirms to me that he views us as merely an unlawful band of troublemakers. Given his attitude and his history, I think it unlikely that he will turn his head and let us fight the Doomen. He fears even the possibility of conflict. Are we so naive as to think he will allow our rebel force to drive out the very beings who gave him rule of this planet—especially knowing that many will demand he be prosecuted for his alliance with the Dominion?"

That said, the room returned to near-chaos. Unhappiness

settled over Melena as she remembered the way things used to be. The Council seldom disagreed and tempers were never lost between each other. And if a Tsuian had given an invitation as Cathra had, there would never have been a reason to mistrust him. Nevertheless, in her mind there was no question: Cathra simply could not be trusted.

"What do you think, Melena?" asked a councilman, holding his pendant and leaning over so he could hear her.

"I think the divisive spirit is Cathra's intent," she sighed, shaking her head. "Why has no one suggested we dismiss and spend more time praying about it?"

But no prayer time came. The meeting lasted late into the night. Some who favored the confrontation persuaded others. Many who were against the meeting wore down in the prolonged discussion and gave in.

Finally Wil rose and addressed the Council and his uncle: "Hud, we agree that Cathra is no longer our friend, and that at the very best he only wants to pacify us with this meeting. But can't we use this meeting to our own advantage? Perhaps it is an opportunity to influence some of those working for Cathra and to get a better idea of the loyalty the Dominion has among our people. And we can determine how many Doomen are stationed in the Palace City."

"All right," said Hud doubtfully, "but I believe it is a terrible mistake—if only for the simple fact that we will be recognizing Cathra as the rightful authority on this planet. Only the Council and the King are the appointed representatives of the Source and the Power in Tsu's government. If we have agreed to go, I insist we go armed and prepared for the worst."

All agreed on that condition and then chose representatives. They also decided to send two of their trained soldiers along. One of those soldiers would be Jern, the young man who had intercepted Cathra's messenger. As the bedraggled leaders left the room, Melena went to Hud and put her arm on his shoulder and gave him a gentle squeeze.

Hud managed a smile and said, "I fear, Melena—"

"A follower of the Source and Power has nothing to fear," she answered. "He is greater than the Dominion, and greater than our own doubts and failings."

Hud loved to see her respond to a challenge—she was so like her father, he thought. "You're right again." Then the long face returned. "I am *concerned*, however, that we may finally be submitting to the Dominion. I feel like Cathra is luring us into a trap. It may well be the end of our movement."

One by one the ten representatives of the underground Council assembled around the massive wooden table once used by the Royal Council when it governed the planet. Many of the underground representatives once had been esteemed members of the Royal Council. Governor Cathra was already seated at the table's head in an elevated seat, dressed in elegant robes and holding a scepter in his hands. Smiling and nodding politely at each representative who entered, Cathra noted that the leaders nodded back but never smiled.

When Hud entered the room, he fired his gaze upon Cathra. The glare pierced Cathra as Hud took his seat.

Wil, seated next to Hud, leaned over and whispered, "Even when my father ruled as King and sat with the Council, he never elevated his seat." Hud nodded, repulsed by the sight.

"I am glad you are all here today," began Cathra, still displaying his grin, "although I can understand it is not a pleasant visit for some of you." Cathra glanced at Hud, but, unnerved by Hud's intense gaze, quickly looked away. "Let us begin by calling on the Source," announced Cathra. He took a deep breath and said ceremoniously, "Source of light and life, be with our gathering and help us arrive at peaceful solutions to the complex problems before us."

During the prayer, Hud surveyed the room. Attendants were all around, standing stiffly at attention: four in each corner; two by the doorway; and one on either side of Cathra. It was obvious they were guards, and were probably armed with concealed weapons.

"Friends," addressed Cathra, "I am aware of your discontent with the present government of Tsu. Your illegal activities these past fifteen years have not gone unnoticed. You apparently misunderstand the situation and it is my intention to enlighten you. We are subjects of the Dominion now. They are powerful, but fair, and we must follow their laws if we are to live in peace."

The underground representatives eyed each other apprehensively; things were not going well. Hud continued to stare at Cathra.

The governor continued, "Now I have discussed matters thoroughly with the representatives of the Dominion. They assure me they will allow us to live our lives in peace, and to practice our religion with only minor restrictions. Surely we agree that the Source would have us live in peace—"

"Pardon me, Cathra," said Hud boldly, rising to his feet, "but we came here to discuss our grievances and to negotiate, not to be filled with your propaganda."

"You are out of order!" flared Cathra. "I command the floor and have not requested your comment!"

"Nor have I requested yours!" exclaimed Hud above Cathra's objections. "You keep insisting on peace when there is no peace. And the Source will not be worshiped here until He is worshiped in purity—not with death dictating how we should—"

"This is *my* meeting, and we shall conduct it with order!" yelled Cathra, leaping to his feet and hitting the table with his scepter.

"With whose order? We did not come to be converted into subjects of the Dominion—"

"Enough!" shouted Cathra, raising his hand. At that signal, two attendants stepped to either side of Hud. "I have heard you out, invited you to a peaceful forum," said Cathra breathlessly, his face flushed. "The people will know that it is I who am trying to be sensible on this planet and you who are instigating trouble for us all!"

Wil leaned back in his seat and shook his head. "So it was a trap all along," he whispered to himself. Discretely reaching into his tunic, he went for his Redlyn pistol. Quick to spot the move, the attendant next to Cathra drew his hidden pistol and fired at Wil. Hud watched in horror as the bolt jolted Wil's body and threw him to the floor clutching his shoulder and gasping.

Each of the ten underground leaders dropped to the ground and drew their weapons. A door behind Cathra's seat opened and Doomen poured in. The first few Doomen were knocked down by Redlyn pistol fire but their comrades jumped over their bodies and continued coming in. Red bolts spliced the air as the

Doomen and the palace guard exchanged fire with the rebels. All around the chamber stone work began crumbling from the random shots, and the Council table splintered and caught fire. More Doomen ran into the Council room and soon outnumbered the underground leaders.

Hud's captors had abandoned him and ran to the other side of the room to guard the door and avoid being accidently shot by the Doomen. In the melee, Hud pulled Jern against the wall.

"This way!" Hud said sharply above the battle. They made their way near the hidden opening through which the Doomen had come and through which Cathra had fled when the first bolt was fired. Hud and Jern chose their marks, pointed their pistols and tore apart the Doomen closest to the opening.

"Get ready to run!" Hud yelled to Jern. Hud then fired his pistol at the main light in the center of the ceiling. The room went dark except for the light of pistol bolts and the small fires they had started. During the brief moments of confusion, Hud and Jern ran for the opening, keeping as low to the ground as possible. Disappearing into the hidden hallway, the Doomen spotted them and began firing. The deafening roar of the bolts tearing into the wall hurt Hud's ears as he yanked the door shut and blasted the opening mechanisn so none could follow.

"You must get back to the base and tell the others what has happened," Hud urged.

"How do we get out of here?" asked Jern, panic in his breathless voice.

"When I was growing up here as a boy, these corridors were used only for maintaining the building. But my brother and I used to chase each other through these tunnels as a game. If we follow this corridor to the end, I think we will reach a door—" Hud cut himself off when they reached the end. Jern stood waiting and listening to the sound of his racing heart pounding in his temples.

"Ah, this is what I was looking for, Jern." He heard a click and Hud slid the door open. Both men shielded their eyes as the daylight poured in.

"This is a ledge which runs around the inside of the palace wall," explained Hud. "I noticed a Doomen on a skip patrolling the courtyard from this ledge. How are you at moving targets?"

"I've been practicing," said Jern eagerly, tightening his grip on his Redlyn pistol.

"Good. Stand here inside the corridor while I watch for the Doomen."

They did not need to wait long before Hud whispered, "Here he comes." Hud dropped behind Jern who was crouched, pointing his pistol at the ledge, waiting for the Doomen to sail past on his skip. They waited several moments but no Doomen came.

"He must have sensed us," said Hud as he drew his pistol and ran out onto the ledge. The Doomen had just stepped off its skip and was planning to investigate when several bolts from Hud's pistol ripped through his body, knocking him from the ledge and sending him tumbling to the ground two stories below. Jern hurried out to meet Hud who was standing by the skip. The vehicle was suspended about waist high from the ground, humming quietly.

"This should get you back safely if you don't attract too much attention," said Hud.

"I'll be fine, but what are you going to do?"

"Make things difficult for the Dominion," Hud answered daringly, reaching into his tunic. He withdrew a pouch and allowed Jern a look.

"Fission detonators!" exclaimed Jern, whistling through his teeth.

"Yes," declared Hud with a satisfied grin. "I had less faith in Cathra than the lot of you." Hud slapped Jern on the back. "Now go!"

Jern swung onto the seat of the sleek vehicle and tested his grip on the handle bar controls.

"The Power guide you," invoked Jern as he pulled his tunic over his mouth. He would be traveling fast, and less wind in his face would make breathing easier.

"And the Source grant you success," replied Hud gently. He watched as Jern accelerated the skip and guided it over the wall, the skip dropped nearly to the ground, then raced from the palace and was soon out of sight. Hud gripped his pistol and slipped back into the corridor.

Chapter Nine

Well, Tsu is straight ahead," announced Lam as Starjumper passed out of the Tsuian light gate. He shook his head once more to clear his mind.

"Home," whispered Maxai, gazing at the bright blue planet.

"It looks as though our first test is coming," warned Lam, breaking the mood. "There's a guard station on the right. And check out what's behind us."

As if on cue, red flashes from the station's gun tower cautioned them they must stop and identify themselves. A Doomen fighter passing by on its orbital patrol escorted Starjumper to the space station. The light gate and the small space station next to it were held in place between the pull of Tsu's gravity and her moon. Lam guided Starjumper near the station, set the com-link on Basic, took a deep breath and addressed the guard.

"We are merchants, trading in Monobarite stones."

The Doomen's dimly lit face filled Starjumper's viewing screen as it routinely demanded, "License."

Lam placed the card into a slot near the command console and soon all the information about his license, age, and history—including a few minor offenses against the Dominion—was transmitted to the station. At first there was no answer.

Lam began to lose courage, but Padu assured him, "We will be allowed through, Lam. Do not worry." Lam rerouted his uneasiness as he slipped his hand into his pocket and fingered his ring while he waited.

"You may pass," rasped the Doomen finally. "Wait for instructions."

"See?" added Padu calmingly to Lam.

"It could be a trap," Lam objected.

Padu's answer was surprisingly stern: "Put away those thoughts, Lam. Remember, your thoughts are not totally your own in the presence of Doomen."

A light on Starjumper's control panel flashed to indicate it was receiving landing instructions, and the ship began its automated descent. It gave Lam a physical sinking feeling that matched his emotional one. This was it—no turning back now. He had willingly flown into the fray. His thoughts flashed back to the port tavern on Saan where the whole mess started.

"I never even got to finish my drink," he muttered, forgetting he had company.

"What was that?" asked Maxai.

"Oh, nothing. My brain hasn't totally re-massed yet, I guess."

Lam watched the controls and Padu threw a tunic at Maxai. "If we call ourselves merchants, we better look the part," suggested Padu. He had already pulled one of Lam's extra tunics over his clothes. The tunics bore the insignia of the merchant's union on their shoulders. Though they were much too small for the Tsuians, they did stretch enough to be passable.

"You'd better strap in," warned Lam. "I don't know how good your landing instructions are here." The planet was entirely surrounded by cloud cover, so the viewing screen remained white as they passed through. Lam dreaded what might lie beyond. His apprehensions faded away with the clouds. When the white began to break up, they could see the lovely continent of Tsu, with its hills and rivers, forests and plains. Soon the Palace City became identifiable, and the buildings appeared to grow larger as they descended. The landing was perfect.

Immediately upon touching the ground, a voice spoke from the com-link: "Governor Cathra welcomes you to the Palace City of Tsu. Please open for boarding and inspection."

Lam released the airlock, opened the hatch and lowered the ramp. The freshness of Tsu's air caught him by surprise. He breathed it deeply as he watched a lone Tsuian guard approach the ship. The guard had only a small pistol strapped to his belt and smiled at them warmly as he entered. Lam, Padu and Maxai stood in the front of the ship and watched the guard make a quick inspection. He made his way around the cabin of the ship, stopping only occasionally to examine the equipment. As he neared the back he stepped with a clank on a piece of loose tile flooring that concealed some of the weapons. Lam caught his breath, his heart in his mouth. The guard stomped on the loose metal with his boot.

"We have a problem here," said the guard. He shook his young head and pointed to the floor. "Someone could get hurt on this. Better get it fixed."

Lam almost burst out laughing, but managed a reserved reply, "Yes, sir, we'll fix it before we leave the planet."

The brief inspection was still much too long for Lam. His alarm had him thinking of his Redlyn pistol as the guard finished and walked back to the airlock. As he passed, the guard looked at Padu. He stopped and searched the older man's face. The guard peered into Padu's kind eyes. The lines around the King's eyes creased into a bright smile; the creaseless forehead of the guard wrinkled into a frown of concentration.

"You remind me of someone . . ." said the guard slowly, searching his mind for the connection.

"A friend, I hope," replied Padu gently.

"Yes—yes, I think so." The guard turned and finally left the ship. Lam and Maxai sighed.

"Thank the Source!" exclaimed Maxai.

"That was close," uttered Lam. "He almost remembered your face."

Padu put a hand on each of his comrade's shoulders and said, "The Source has his hand on us. Now, let's make arrangements to unload this cargo."

Lam, Padu and Maxai stood under a tent near a street in the city. The man with whom they were speaking was not moving his lips; they knew they had gotten his best price.

"Thirty-five Quoaro a piece then," groaned Padu. "We just won't eat for a while." The man with whom they had been bargaining now smiled and unfolded his hands.

"They are fine craft," he said. "I know you will be happy with them. There are no finer skips on Tsu—riding them is like hitching a ride on a thought."

"Enough, enough, friend," laughed Padu. "There's no need to sell them to us twice."

The trio walked beside their new vehicles, guiding them to a shady spot nearby where Padu outlined their plans.

"Maxai will travel through the city and, if possible, determine the strength of the Doomen presence here. You should also talk to people and try to discern their mood. Pick up any news that might be relevant to us. Then return to the ship and guard our cargo. Lam and I will travel to the place where I believe those loyal to the Source will be hiding."

They strapped on their helmets and mounted their skips. Lam struggled to swing his still-splinted leg over his skip's seat.

"Be courageous and careful, and the Power guide you," Padu called to Maxai.

"Take care yourself," cautioned Maxai. "You are the one in the most danger here." Padu smiled and then motioned for Lam to follow him. Padu swung his skip around and sped off, hardly hesitating at corners.

Soon the buildings gave way to countryside. Padu set his skip to ride higher and warned Lam to do the same. Then he pushed his heel against the speed control and shot ahead. Lam had all he could do to stay close. He had never ridden a Tsuian skip, although they were similar to the skips he and his friends had raced as boys. They were the fastest vehicles a person could safely ride on the planet's surface, but at these speeds even they were not safe.

Lam fumbled to pull down his visor so he could see without squinting and breathe. They were on a country road, and occasionally a branch from a tree near the road would slap their skips. Other than that it was a smooth trip, and could have even been pleasant had Padu not run his skip wide open.

Warning lights on Padu's skip meant he was slowing down. Lam followed him just off the road under one of Tsu's tall, thin trees.

"Our destination lies off the road and up the mountain," said Padu, lifting his visor. "It is still some distance and I will be traveling fast and low to avoid detection. Just try to follow me exactly and you should avoid any hazards."

"I'll be fine. I grew up on one of these."

"Yes, but I grew up on this mountain." Padu winked, closed his visor and sped off. Lam kicked his skip into high range and clumsily lowered his visor while he steered.

It was not long before they were in the foothills, careening around jagged rock formations and hopping over sparkling streams. Lam wished Padu would stop for a long drink of such pure water. His ears began to feel the pressure as they climbed the mountain and the air was cooling. Then, he saw Padu slowing down and signaling him to pull alongside.

Padu pulled up his visor and shouted above the wind, "Do you see that cave?" he pointed to an area of mountain that had a ledge and a few scattered boulders.

"No, where is it?"

"Good, then it is well hidden." He shut his visor and urged his skip forward to the ledge. When Lam reached the ledge, Padu had already dismounted and removed his helmet.

"Thousands of years ago, this cave was a Monobarite mine. My brother and I used to pretend this was our palace when we were young. The last thing he said to me before I fled the planet was, 'I'll meet you at our mountain palace.' I believe we will find friends here."

Lam dismounted and they walked their skips through the jumble of boulders.

"There it is," said Padu, pointing to the large black hole in the mountain's side. *Not exactly what you'd call home*, thought Lam. They turned on the lights of their skips so they could see their path better.

"What!" gasped Lam as their lights illuminated a soldier standing before them with his pistol pointed at Padu's head.

"Hands on your head," the guard commanded, "and walk slowly this way." He motioned with his head that they should enter the cave. Lam and Padu unquestioningly proceeded, Lam attempting to favor his broken leg. The guard pulled out a pocket com-link and spoke into it.

"Jern here. I'm bringing in two prisoners."

The end of the tunnel opened into a hangar where two people were waiting. Melena was one of them. She had not gone to the fateful meeting, but had stayed to help lead the group in case something happened to the representatives. Jern had returned only hours before and reported the dreadful news about the sabotage at the meeting. Too anxious to rest, he had volunteered to guard the entrance.

Light spilled on the prisoners, and Lam and Padu squinted as their eyes adjusted. Melena's eyes widened in disbelief.

"Father!" she shrieked and ran to him. She threw her arms around him and began to sob, then gave way to tears. Padu gave a shout of laughter and returned her embrace. His eyes glistened with tears. Jern dropped his pistol to his side and moved back in awe.

He lowered himself to one knee and said, "*Ma Arna!*"

"Being marched at gunpoint is a strange welcome for a king," Padu joked, but then put his hand on Jern's shoulder. "You did your job well."

The other man with Melena turned, cupped his hands over his mouth and yelled, "The King has returned!" The jubilant shout was echoed by several others, and soon nearly everyone from the underground colony surrounded the King, thanking the Source and buzzing with questions. Here was new hope for their present darkness.

"Words cannot express all the joy I feel at being home with you again," exulted the King. "During my absence, the Power has revealed to me that Tsu is destined to be the birthplace of the first successful rebellion against the Dominion." At those words a cheer went up from the two hundred gathered in the hangar area.

"The spread of their evil is great—they swallow planet after planet and rule them by fear, violence and death. But we will be the first crack in the Dominion, and the genesis of its eventual downfall!" Shouts of applause drowned out the King, as years of frustration gave way to joy.

Melena and Padu soon dismissed the crowds, and then met with Jern and Lam in the Council room.

"Now tell me what has just happened," said Padu to Melena.

Melena's heart was lighter now that her father was present, even as she related the distressing news. "Jern has just returned from the Palace City, Father. Some of our leaders went to the palace to meet with Cathra, who is now governor under the

Dominion. Cathra deceived us into thinking he wanted to work with us or to negotiate, but it was a Doomen ambush. After a fight, our leaders were all imprisoned except for your brother."

Padu nodded gravely.

"And sire," Jern said quietly, "Wil was wounded in the fight. He was alive when I left—I don't know how badly he was hurt."

They sat in silence, as the king turned the matter over in his mind. Finally he asked Melena, "How many soldiers do we have?"

"Two hundred altogether. But only one hundred fifty of us are trained in pistols. About thirty of us are trained as pilots and flight crew."

"Ships and arms?"

"We have the old carrier we salvaged—that's in its own hangar. Out here we have eighteen fighters. I'm afraid we have guns on only about half of them, and those are only small Redlyn blasters. We had only about forty Redlyn pistols, but nine were lost in the skirmish at the palace. Oh, and we have a few fission detonators. That's about it."

"Obviously we must act quickly—our friends are prisoners of the Dominion. We cannot lose them or any more time," urged Padu. "Do you have spare gravity resistors?"

"We have several that we use to haul parts in the hangar," answered Melena.

"Good. I want at least two large gravity resisting platforms made, large enough to hold twenty people each. We will pull them behind skips. Paint them brightly and prepare banners with the royal crest and symbols of our faith. And, are there any musicians here?"

"Yes," observed Melena. "Many."

"Good. Assemble them also. I will travel to both of the other major cities and announce that I have returned. I believe many will desire to follow us. Send enough soldiers to prevent an immediate, small-scale attack. The Doomen will need time to group together, and to catch up with us before they can do anything. By that time I expect we will be ready to put up a fair fight. We can discuss this more in a short while. Could we be ready by morning?"

Jern jumped to his feet and said, "We'll begin right away!"

"Wait," said Padu, cheered by Jern's enthusiasm. "In the Palace City port is a merchant ship belonging to our friend, Lam. On it you will find Maxai the ambassador."

"Maxai!" exclaimed Melena joyfully.

"Yes," laughed Padu. "You will also find enough weapons to finish arming your fighters and soldiers." At the news Jern clapped his hands together for joy. "Take a group of men in twos, dressed as we are; enter the ship and transport the arms back here. Jern, I want you to take a small group to the palace to find out what can be done about our people there."

Jern and Melena hurried out to fulfill Padu's instructions.

Padu turned to Lam and said, "Now it is time for me to do something for you for a change. Let's find the medical station and get you something to help you walk." Lam and Padu began walking through the already frantically busy underground. Lam limped along as fast as he could.

"They have accomplished much in fifteen years," remarked Padu.

"It's quite a place," admitted Lam. He was thinking about the danger involved in their plan and wondered why he was going along with it. The more he thought about it, the crazier it appeared. Maybe it was partly because of Padu—his firm gentleness was beginning to win Lam over. Before he could hardly wait to get away; now Lam feared they might not have much more time together. Deep within arose a desire to let down his defenses and reveal the truth about himself to Padu.

"Here it is," announced Padu as they reached the room marked "Medical" in Tsuian. Padu entered first; Lam hesitated. They would be alone so this might be a good time to talk. Padu was the first person Lam had met in years whom he felt he might be able to trust fully. The full weight of Lam's emotions took hold of him. He took a deep breath and followed.

"One of these should do well," noted Padu, looking over a rack with a small selection of walking sticks.

"Padu," said Lam after a hard swallow. Padu glanced over his shoulder at Lam.

"Yes?"

"There are many things I'd like to talk with you about. I'm not sure where to start."

Padu nodded understandingly and motioned for Lam to sit on one of the cots. Padu sat on a cot nearby.

"I have seen so many strange things lately—coincidences," said Lam, looking away from Padu. "I don't believe in the supernatural, but I can't dismiss your, and Max's, faith. It seems so real to you, and I've never experienced anything like this."

"Do you doubt your firmly held conviction that there is no power but what can be seen?"

"I guess I do."

"Then the Power is at work in you. If you put your trust in Him, He will become more real to you than the world you can see."

Lam nodded in response. Padu's answer did not solve anything, but at least Lam's doubts were in the open.

"One of the strange things I was talking about," continued Lam, struggling to speak the words, "is that I feel I have to tell you about who and what I am. It hasn't been since I was a boy that I felt I could trust anyone."

Padu waited quietly for Lam to look at him. Then the King said gently, "You are Entarian, aren't you."

Lam's gaze dropped to the floor and he nodded.

"I'm sorry, Lam."

"I was training to be a merchant on Entar fifteen years ago. I had just left on my first apprentice flight. We were carrying food to a space station between Saan and the Ante Demarian system when I got the news. The commander at the station refused to even look at me; he just handed me a copy of the report and walked away. They should have arrested me, but they didn't. I guess they felt sorry for a kid like me.

"I read the report and I couldn't believe it. I wouldn't believe it! My master and I did not speak all the way back to Entar. We could tell even upon descent that the report was true. Where the gleam of our cities should have been, there were horrible black scars. And we could see forest fires and grass burning everywhere around the cities—or what was left of them.

"We landed on the cracked pavement of the spaceport. It was difficult to find a place to touch down between the wreckage. As soon as the door opened I ran out. Not a building was left standing. It was nearly impossible to tell it was the same city I had grown up in.

"My family lived near the spaceport so I ran off in that direction. I stepped over broken glass and stone. I wended my way between fallen signs and the charred remains of trees. I stood where our shop had been. There was nothing but ashes and rubble. The horror of it impacted me and I began digging with my bare hands to find a body, or at least an artifact. I dug till my hands bled. There was nothing. The Dominion had wiped away my entire life. Everything and everyone I loved. Gone."

Padu listened in silence and nodded. Tears once more filled these gentle eyes. Lam took out the ring he carried in his pocket. "This is all I have. The girl I had been dating gave me this before I left. She said it would help me to remember her." Tears began to flow from Lam's eyes for the first time in many bitter years. He paused a moment before he was able to continue.

"I sat on some stones overlooking the remains of my city. I couldn't comprehend my loss. I sat until the sun began to set and the air chilled. I had no idea of what I would do. I finally got up and picked my way back to the port. When I got there, my master was speaking with some men from a ship that had just landed. They were pirates who had come to loot the city. They asked us to come with them and join the Cartel, so I did. I had nothing else to turn to. I did well in my apprenticeship with them. In fact, they gave me Starjumper."

Padu spoke gently, "So you are a pirate. And the license?"

"Phoney. I tried to discourage you, but—"

Padu did not let him finish. "It worked, didn't it?" Lam laughed.

"But I want you to know, Padu, that I only attacked Dominion vessels, and intentionally killed only Doomen."

Padu placed his hand on Lam's shoulder, as he said firmly and reassuringly, "What you did in the past is not important to me. The Power is stirring in you now, and I know that your life will be different. You will need to deal with your past, but you have to understand that need first. For now, please take this." Padu handed him a slender walking stick from the small rack nearby. "It is made from the heart of the Ching tree. It is as strong as many metals and much lighter."

Lam broke into a broad grin and said, "Thanks for everything." He took a deep breath and added, "We've got a lot of work to do. We'd better get to it."

Chapter Ten

Cathra nearly choked on his food when he heard.

"The King? Here?" he gasped. He turned pale, then flushed with anger. The palace guard's commander who stood slightly bowed before him was flooded with accusing questions, "When? How?"

"We don't know, Governor Cathra, but according to our sources on the East Coast, he is traveling with an armada and rallying the people against the Dominion."

Cathra's normally large appetite now eluded him. He pushed away his food, rose from the table, and began pacing.

"Shall I alert the Doomen?" asked the commander.

"Certainly not!" Cathra declared with panic in his voice. "It would be the end of Tsu—and you and me. We have to handle this ourselves. How many are with him?"

"Reports vary, but between twenty and twenty-five."

"We should be able to contain them. Take the entire palace guard, except for a few to watch the wall and guard the prisoners. Go at once and capture the King—and avoid bloodshed if possible; we have enough problems already."

When the commander of the guard left, Cathra stood at his open window and observed the commotion as the palace guard prepared to capture Padu and his retinue. Cathra felt very secure in his room overlooking the courtyard. From here he felt he could observe and control all that went on. From his youth he had disagreed with the policies of the elders and when he finally gained eldership, he had taken advantage of it.

"What do you hope to accomplish, Padeus?" Cathra muttered to himself. He listened as the officer barked orders and the palace guard assembled in the courtyard. "You will only bring the wrath of the Dominion upon our planet and likely destroy us all. Why must you constantly struggle against things you cannot change? Why don't you keep your radical beliefs to yourself and let the rest of us live in peace?"

When the palace guard sped off in their armed skips, Cathra left his window vigil and returned to the table. He swallowed the last of his drink. It seemed to warm him. His mind wandered to the last Council meeting before the Doomen finally occupied the entire planet. "The Dominion embodies death. Life and death cannot live together on the same planet!" Padeus had pronounced.

Cathra laughed dryly. "If it had not been for me," he savored to himself, "we would have all been dead."

Cathra refilled his goblet, took another swallow and amazed himself with other magestic thoughts.

"There are only four hours of darkness left," warned Lam. Maxai stretched, and then tried rolling his head to get rid of the kinks he had acquired while sleeping in one of the Starjumper's seats.

"How many came with you?" yawned Maxai.

"Oh, a few," Lam replied, pulling up floor tiles. "We thought we'd take loads by twos into the woods so it would appear like the original three merchants that came in Starjumper."

"Sounds good," said Maxai, helping Lam extract Redlyn pistols from the hidden compartments. "Tell me what happened when you and Padu got to the underground base."

Lam laughed and said, "They were so excited I think they could have taken over the Dominion barehanded. We departed as soon as Padu left on his tour of other cities to rally support. He had musicians playing and banners flying—it was the wildest maneuver I've ever seen. Meanwhile we sort of sneaked out the back way. I mean I felt wierd traveling with these guys all dressed like me—sort of a gang of merchants. If I wasn't scared to death, this would be pretty funny!"

"But you didn't have any trouble?" wondered Maxai.

"Not yet. Your people here are no strangers to smuggling.

They have a hidden trail cut into the woods that leads right up here to the north edge of the space port. I've never seen anything like this. They've even cut a nice neat gate in the fence. Can you believe that? I guess they run a lot of provisions for the underground that way."

The job went slowly, working in twos as they carried their cargo into the woods, left it, and then returned for more. The cannons were especially difficult to move. Lam nearly worried himself sick, constantly fearing they would be spotted. No lie would bail them out of this jam. But the hours passed and it appeared they went unnoticed. As the sky began to lighten, they took the last load into the woods. They mounted the cannons between skips and packed the skips' storage compartments. Maxai was the last one into the woods. He joined the rest in the skip they had bought in town the day before. Lam did not have as much storage on his skip as the others, so he had tucked pistols in his trousers and, with torn rags, had strapped some under his skip's seat.

"The sky is lightening up," urged Lam. "We'll have to travel fast."

"Just follow us," waved the driver of the lead skip. "And be careful, we will be going fast."

"Yeah. I know how you people drive around here," said Lam wryly, remembering his wild ride following Padu up the mountain.

They each pushed their skips to high range and the dust from the road rose behind them. Lam was second in line and Maxai followed him as they traveled in the twilight along the quiet country road. Only the faint sounds of insects could be heard beside the sound of air rushing past their skips. The light from Palace City and the stars grew fainter as the sunlight spread over the horizon. Lam was delighted they were putting a good distance between themselves and the port.

Just when Lam's anxiety level was growing less acute, he heard a loud, grinding crash behind him. He turned to see Maxai's skip sliding on the dirt. Maxai struggled to control it, but it finally tumbled and he was thrown to the ground. The skips behind it nearly lost control as they swerved to avoid colliding with the crashed skip. Lam turned around and drove up beside the fallen driver. Maxai was sitting up, checking himself for injuries.

"You okay, Max?" asked Lam from his skip.

"It looks like it, but it doesn't feel like it."

Turning to the others, Lam suggested, "I'll stay and help Max get his skip back up if you guys want to head back."

"That's probably the best idea," answered Jern. "The crews will want to get these cannons on the fighters as soon as possible."

The others wished them well and then sped off. Lam guided his skip to the fallen vehicle and dismounted. Maxai picked himself up and joined the examination of the skip's mechanisms.

"It looks like the regulator for the gravity resistor has broken leads. What do you think?" asked Lam.

"That's certainly what it felt like. This model really goes through the leads in a hurry. I guess I should have checked it when we bought it. There should be a spare one in here." Maxai rummaged through the tool case under the seat. He produced the needed part and they worked quickly to install it.

"That should do it," announced Maxai, brushing the dirt off his clothes with his hands.

"Good. Let's go!" shouted Lam, hobbling quickly toward his own skip. "There are lights behind us!"

The men accelerated their skips and shot down the road. The vehicle behind them spotted them and fired a red warning bolt into the sky. Lam and Maxai leaned forward to cut wind resistance. They had a good lead, but did not want to lead whoever was chasing them back to the underground. Lam's heart was racing as fast as his skip as he looked back to see how Maxai was doing. Maxai motioned for him to pull into the woods to their left. Lam nodded and followed his lead. They almost crashed as they plunged wildly into the woods, but regained control and pulled to a stop. They sat soundlessly and listened to the patrol rush past.

"This is a good way to go, anyway," smiled Maxai.

"Is there any possibility of you going faster?" Lam smirked.

Reaching the underground, they found a beehive of activity.

The echoes of hammers and torches fought each other in the hangar, and people ran back and forth in the halls. Crews were installing cannons on the weaponless fighters, and soldiers were practicing with their new Redlyn pistols.

"I'm so happy you made it back safely," called Melena running up to Lam and Maxai. She gave them each a hug; with that welcome, Lam thought that it was especially good to be back.

"Lam," asked Melena, "could you help us test our fighter engines? They've never been flown, and we can't afford any problems when we do."

"Sure," he answered, picking up his walking stick from the runner of his skip and wondering what condition he would find the fighters in. "But maybe you could first tell me where a guy could get something to wash the dust out of his throat."

In a small cell in the basement of the palace, one of the older Council members checked the makeshift bandages on Wil's injured arm. Wil was not fully conscious and winced occasionally from pain.

"He's doing better," he announced after examining the wounds. Quiet exclamations of "Praise to the Source" passed around the cell. The councilman stood up, straightened his robe and walked to the entrance of the cell which was blocked with a gate—a feature of the palace contributed by the Doomen. As he stood he had heard the sound of voices raised in song, first quietly, then louder as more of the underground prisoners being held nearby began to sing. Soon they were all singing the same song, a joyful praise song about the strength of the Source and the Power.

The guard was flustered by the commotion and tried to quiet them down, but the singing only grew louder. He finally yelled something into the com-link on the wall. Soon Cathra came huffing down the steps. Summoned by the guard, Cathra went to each cell and raised his hands, pleading for and then demanding silence, but to no avail. He gave up this futility, deciding instead to discuss with the guard which rebel to "discipline" as an example to the others.

The cells did not quiet down until the commander of the

palace guard came stumbling down the steps and threw himself at Cathra's feet for mercy.

"Explain yourself," demanded Cathra of the heap on the floor.

"Our mission has failed, Governor Cathra!" cried the commander between gasps.

"What do you mean?" screamed Cathra hoarsely, turning pale.

"There are not twenty-five of them as we thought; there are over a thousand. They follow the King on skips and transports, in ships and vehicles of various sizes, and even on foot—they are armed and coming here to the Palace City."

Cathra stared open-mouthed at the man on the floor. Seconds later, victory shouts came from the prisoners who had been listening to the whole thing. "The King has returned!"

Even Wil stood up and stumbled to the grate, grabbing it with his good arm to avoid falling.

"Begin to pray for mercy, Cathra," panted Wil. Cathra glared at Wil, then the commander; he whirled and stamped up the stairs.

Chapter Eleven

The roar was deafening. The sound of the fighter's engine vibrated through the hangar while the crew members nearby covered their ears. Lam, standing on the ground, waved his arms to the technician in the fighter; the noise ceased.

"That should do it," Lam yelled up to the technician. "That's the last one, isn't it?"

"That's it," the technician shouted back.

Lam felt a tap on his shoulder. He turned and faced Maxai.

"We just heard from the King again, Lam," he informed him. "Each report indicates an astonishing success. It seems as if the entire population of Tsu is following him."

"Great," said Lam half-heartedly. "But did he say what we're supposed to do next?" That was Lam's latest anxiety. Each passing hour and each call from Padu made him more apprehensive. A fight was coming—and he wanted to be prepared, but didn't know what to do. While Maxai answered, Lam walked over to the fighter whose engines had just been tested, picked up a wrench and started loosening the floor brackets that kept the fighter from taking off when its engines fired.

"Yes," answered Maxai. "Padu says the Doomen patrols from the cities have fled in their ships. We believe they are grouping at the orbiting station to prepare for a consolidated attack."

Sweat ran down Lam's temples as he vented his anxiety on a stubborn bolt. "Why haven't they attacked already?" asked Lam between grunts.

"They're probably waiting for the King and his followers to reach the Palace City so they can concentrate their attack. He'll be here shortly after daybreak."

The bolt Lam strained at creaked as if it were begging for

79

mercy. Finally the wrench swung and Lam, victorious, shook the cramps out of his arms.

"But what are we supposed to do?" he demanded.

"Padu wants our fighters to meet the Doomen in space—and take them out—before he reaches the Palace City," pronounced Maxai. Then putting his hand on Lam's shoulder he added, "He'd like you to lead the attack because you are the most qualified."

Lam did not reply right away. He looked at Maxai; the ambassador looked like a fighter mechanic now. Lam was caught square in the middle. He couldn't imagine anyone else being asked to lead the fighters, but he knew from experience that Doomen fighters didn't just hang in space waiting to be shot down by inexperienced flight teams.

"I'll do it," declared Lam. "If I can fly Starjumper," he quickly added.

"Don't you think it's risky to take off from a guarded port?"

"It didn't seem to be heavily guarded," Lam observed sarcastically, remembering the easy time they had smuggling the weapons. "Besides," he gestured at the fighter behind him, "I can't even read the controls on these things. They're in Tsuian. Which is riskier?"

"Hmm, I guess you're right," admitted Maxai.

"What about your buddies in the palace?"

"We have no report yet, but we figure Cathra will use them as a bargaining tool when the King retakes the city. Padu thinks we should rescue them."

"That's all he said? He's off cruising the countryside and here we are. Didn't he offer any suggestions on how to do that?"

"Well, no—but Jern and I are somewhat familiar with the palace, and the King's brother, Hud, may still be free in the palace. If Jern and I could take a team with us—especially if we found Hud—we should be able to free them."

"Okay," deliberated Lam after some thought. "I'll go with you to the city. You take care of the others and I'll take Starjumper. Your fighters can take off to the side of Tsu opposite the space station. I'll meet them there and we should surprise them—you said the Doomen don't know about the fighters. We'll try to make it easy for Padu."

Lam, Jern, Maxai and six others abandoned their skips in the woods just outside the Palace City. They hugged the walls for cover as they moved cautiously toward the palace. Lam massaged his eyes and stifled a yawn. The few hours sleep he had managed seemed only to make him more tired. *If I survive this one, I think I'll park on an asteroid and sleep for a decade*, he mused.

"The city seems deserted," whispered Lam to Maxai.

"Strange, isn't it? I think most everyone went to the country yesterday to meet the King."

Lam looked to the sky almost expecting to see Doomen fighters bearing down on them. It was not as dark as it had been, but wisps of fog still swirled around their feet as they passed through the empty street. Soon the sun would be above the mountains and would burn off the fog; then it would be more difficult to travel unnoticed.

"There!" breathed Jern, pointing to the palace tower now visible above the buildings of the city. The first rays of sun were already touching the twisting serpent depicted on a banner hanging from a pole on the tower. As the group approached, they could see the wall and something that made their hearts sink. Twenty-five Tsuian guards lined the wall—some talking to each other, others surveying the city.

"They must have the whole palace guard up there!" exclaimed Jern in dismay.

"I expected them to be at the edge of the city waiting to meet the King's assault—or fleeing in fear," said Maxai shaking his head.

"We're outnumbered," admitted Jern, "but we've been training for this for years."

They stood and stared at the wall for a few moments. The sun was climbing, and soon they would lose their shadow cover.

Lam finally broke the indecision, "I'll run down to the south a little ways and try to knock the top of that tower off. That should be a good enough distraction for you to advance to one of those alcoves in the wall."

Without waiting for agreement, Lam crouched and dashed as fast as he could with his limping leg. He crossed the street and looked at the guards. They had not noticed him yet. Slipping between the buildings and then ducking around the corner, he leaned against the wall and lifted his pistol. He took careful aim, knowing that if he missed, they would be attracted to him instead of the tower and the precious seconds the others needed to reach the wall would be lost. The entire mission might fail if he missed.

Lam inhaled deeply and then slowly let out half his air. He touched back on the activator.

"What are you doing there?" demanded an old woman's voice behind him. He whirled around and saw that he was being threatened by a cobweb cleaning stick. "Up to no good, I can see that!" she crackled as she wielded her domestic weapon.

Lam could understand little of her Tsuian language, but he motioned for her to be quiet as he glanced at the palace to make sure her commotion had not attracted the guards' attention. One of them seemed to be looking his way.

"It didn't use to be this way!" she shrieked, hitting Lam with her stick. "People didn't go sneaking around a helpless woman's house with guns. Why, when Padeus was King—"

Lam recognized the word "Padeus," so he repeated it. The woman stopped her attack for a moment out of respect for the name.

"I—with Padeus," Lam enunciated in the best Tsuian he could piece together from the fragments he had picked up. "Padeus—is—come."

"Oh, you're with the King!" she screeched with delight. "And I thought I would miss him." Then to Lam's dismay, she left the shelter of the building and marched as fast toward the wall as her ancient legs would carry her, brandishing her stick and shouting at the guards to give up before it was too late. Lam shook his head, certain his element of surprise had melted away. But soon all the guards were gathering closer to the tower to watch the old woman scolding them. He watched Maxai and Jern's group approach the wall unnoticed.

"She's hired!" he declared to himself, grinning. He, too, took advantage of the distraction and moved further south along the wall to the other side of the tower. Seeing the stairs unguarded, he quickly slipped up to them.

One of Jern's team whirled a grapnel and rope until it hummed, then slung it up to the top of the wall. The hook was coated with a soft material so it made little noise. Each of the others did the same while Maxai, not being in as good condition, stayed below to cover them. Moments later each of the underground team had dropped noiselessly to the ledge.

The palace guards were totally absorbed in mocking the old woman below. Three of them felt it first: Redlyn pistol points held against their backs.

"Do not touch your weapons," commanded Jern. "Do not move. In the name of the Source and the Power, and in the name of King Padeus, I command you to raise your arms slowly above your head. You are our prisoners."

The guards obeyed and slowly peered around. Jern and three others stood to the north of them with their pistols raised. Lam was now to their south. Several other underground soldiers had crept to the tower and were ready to pick off any guard that dared to move. One of the underground with Jern weaved among the crowd of guards and confiscated their weapons.

"Don't worry," said Jern to the disarmed guards who stood trembling in their boots. "You are safe unless you give us reason to shoot. Your lives depend not upon us, but the mercy of the King."

Lam joined Jern and addressed him quietly, "You don't dare leave too few of your people here to guard our prisoners. Do you feel like rescuing an underground Council with me?"

"I can't wait," asserted Jern eagerly. He called Maxai up to take charge while Jern and Lam walked briskly along the ledge to the hidden passage Jern had used in his escape. The triumphant old woman went back to her house exhausted, apparently confident that matters were in the proper hands.

Lam and Jern slipped along the ledge, and when they reached the corner of the palace wall, they flattened themselves against the smooth, brown stones of the corner tower.

"I would be surprised if all the guards were on one wall," whispered Jern.

"I'm ready," answered Lam, gripping his pistol tighter. Jern made his move and safely reached the spot with the small brown door that blended in with the stone. Following close behind, Lam kept his eyes open for any guards.

"This is it," noted Jern, "but I don't see a knob or a switch anywhere."

Jern ran his hand along the door and the stone around it while Lam bent over and checked for a loose stone on the floor that might conceal a switch. He found nothing, but before he could straighten up, the door slid open and a robed figure towered above him with a raised pistol. Lam's heart stopped and he began to raise his hands in surrender. To his astonishment, Jern stepped to the man and embraced him. *What in the galaxy?* wondered Lam.

"What took you so long?" asked Hud.

"I'm sorry," explained Jern with mock contrition, "but we had to capture the palace guard first." Hud pulled the two into the corridor and slid the door shut, leaving them in total darkness. Jern introduced Lam as they followed the twisting path through the interior of the palace. *So much for introductions,* Lam figured. It was not long before Lam had lost all sense of direction.

"We must be quiet now," warned Hud; "we are nearing the detention area." A door scraped open, and they cautiously stepped into the dimly lit hall. Even the dim light made them blink after having groped so long in the dark. They walked quietly, pistols raised and bodies flattened against the wall.

Nearing a corner, Hud whispered, "The prisoners will probably be guarded by only one attendant. If we surprise him together, I think he can be persuaded to surrender." Lam and Jern prepared to leap around the corner with Hud. "Now!" he whispered.

The three of them jumped out into the hallway and crouched with their pistols raised. The guard sat, half dozing, with his back to them. The gallant rescuers looked at each other.

Lam asked the others, "Who wants to tell him?"

Startled, the guard jerked, picked up his pistol and swung around. His face turned from amazement to despair as he looked into the three pistol points. Jern stepped forward and relieved him of his weapons, then pushed the buttons on the wall that unlocked the grates in front of the cells. Hud and Jern opened doors for the prisoners as Lam kept his weapon trained on the dumfounded guard.

"What a way to wake up," marveled one Council member,

rubbing his eyes. "I should sleep more often!"

"I would like everyone to meet our new friend, Lam Laeo," announced Hud to the assembly of yawning and stretching underground leaders. "He came with King Padeus." Several of them hugged him or slapped him gently on the back.

"I knew we would be rescued," expressed a gentle-looking woman, trying to straighten her crumpled robes. "You are an answer to prayer, Lam." Lam wasn't sure how an answer to prayer should act, so he just nodded and smiled.

Jern had entered Wil's cell and was helping him up. "How are you doing?" Jern asked.

"Much better," Wil answered weakly. "You know us Tsuians—we don't stay down long. But getting up still makes me dizzy." Jern let Wil lean on him as they entered the hallway.

"Friends," Hud spoke quietly to the group gathered in the corridor, "I am glad to be with you again. But now that you are in capable hands, I must leave you again for a while."

"Wait a minute!" Jern exclaimed. "How do we get out of here?"

"Just follow this corridor until you reach a stairway. Go up the stairs to the first landing, then take the far door. The stairs there will lead you to one of the southern towers where you can join our subdued friends on the wall."

"Isn't it dangerous for you here?" asked Lam, who wasn't sure who Hud was.

Hud laughed, "Friend, I know my way around this maze nearly as well as the mice do. The Power guide you." With that he disappeared again into the walls.

Lam led the group single file up the stairs. Not sure of what to expect, he leaned heavily on his walking stick with one hand and kept his pistol raised with the other. This many people could not possibly be as quiet as Lam wished they would be. Spotting the landing, he knew there should be a door on the far side that would lead them to the safety of their group on the wall. He reached the landing and turned the corner.

"Well, well," taunted Cathra angrily, his arms folded and his cold eyes staring at the fugitives. "Out for a walk?"

The guard in front of Cathra commanded Lam, "Drop your weapon."

"I'm sorry, I don't understand Tsuian very well," he stated plainly in Common. The guard held his pistol to Lam's face, and Lam decided he could tell from the context what the guard wanted. "Okay," he continued in Common, "here it is!" Lam tossed his pistol at the guard's foot and the guard looked down as the weapon bounced on the floor. Swinging his walking stick, Lam connected on the guard's jaw with a resounding crack. Cathra, mouth open in astonishment, turned in typical fashion to run. Jern had leaped past the once-again free prisoners to chase Cathra. Lam disarmed the unconscious guard and watched as Jern caught Cathra by the robe and jerked him off his feet. It was a moment they had all waited for. When Cathra looked up, Jern's pistol was in his cowardly face.

"Do you think there are any more guards around here?" asked Lam, meeting Jern on the landing.

"I hope not," he said with a tired voice.

Reaching the top of the stairs, the group entered a circular room where a skip was stored for the guards' rounds. Jern ran to the window and looked down. His comrades still stood with pistols pointed at the palace guard. As they descended the stairs to the ledge, it seemed to Lam there were fewer prisoners. He could see a harrowed look on the faces of some of the underground soldiers.

"Max," asked Lam, scrutinizing the distressed guards, "do we have a prisoner missing, or did I miscount?"

Maxai sighed, "I can hardly believe it, but the commander of the guard threw himself off the wall. He died instantly." Maxai shook his head remorsefully. When he had left Tsu as an ambassador, suicide was unheard of among his people.

Jern suddenly tugged on Lam's arm and said quietly but urgently, "You have your own mission. I'm grateful for your help—in fact, I completely forgot about your task in the excitement. But it's getting later in the morning, and I wonder if the battle might be won but the war jeopardized."

Lam's forehead furrowed. Tucking his pistol into his belt, he hurried up the stairs, almost forgetting the pain in his leg. He burst through the door and swung onto the skip. He eased it out onto the ramp that led to the ledge on the other side of the tower, then kicked it into high range past the ledge and over the wall. It dropped quickly but stopped short of the ground and sped toward the spaceport in a graceful but stomach-turning manuever.

Lam traveled the empty street at top speed, squinting and gasping for air, in his haste having neglected a helmet. He tried to concentrate only on his driving but kept worrying that he had spent far too much time in the palace. If the King were to march into the Palace City now, the Doomen would swoop down on the helpless city and utterly destroy it with fire from their fighters.

It seemed strange traveling through the deserted city in daylight. He was sure the inhabitants were either hiding or gone to the country to meet the King. It made him feel alone and anxious.

Soon Lam sighted the spaceport control towers. He did not watch for guards, hoping they were gone along with the rest of the people. Hoping did not change the facts. Several red flashes from the Tsuian guard at the port gate missed him but dashed his plans for an easy escape.

Lam swerved and dipped to dodge the bolts as he tried to decide if he could control the skip with one hand and shoot with the other. He did not have time to decide—he was too close. Instinctively he banked his skip so that the bottom faced the guard, hoping he could come out of the turn right after he passed the guard and then bank the other direction through the gate. He knew if he went straight through the gate, the guard would pick him off like a practice target, and the fence was too tall for a skip to jump at close range.

His plan failed. As the bottom of his skip faced the guard, the man fired and landed a direct hit on Lam's gravity resistor. The skip hit the ground and Lam dove clear, landing roughly on the pavement. His skip, now rolling and in flames, collided with the guardhouse and exploded. Shaking his head to clear it, Lam propped himself up on his scraped arm and used his other hand to shield his eyes from the heat of the flames. *Either that skip or that guardhouse had explosives*, mused Lam. Then he remembered Starjumper.

"I'm coming, girl," he said audibly as he struggled to his feet. He retrieved his walking stick, which had been thrown from the skip. He then limped, feeling as though every limb in his body was crippled, to where his ship rested, gleaming white in the morning sun. As he neared it, his strength began to return. Her ramp was down and the hatch was open, as was the custom when foreign ships were at port—it was a sign of goodwill. In this case it meant he could leave more quickly. Climbing the ramp and throwing himself into his seat, he did not even wait to program a launch sequence. He closed the hatch and retrieved the ramp with the manual override, then started the engines. Suddenly the unimaginable appeared.

Through the viewing port he could see them. They leveled shoulder blasters at Starjumper and began firing. Doomen!

"I thought you were all in space!" he yelled. The blasters couldn't do much to Starjumper, but Lam could see two Doomen fighters on the ground behind the soldiers. Not only would they follow him, but now their partners in orbit would know he was coming. The ships were too close to shoot with Starjumper's guns; an explosion at that range would cripple his ship too. There was nothing else to do. He heaved on the manual guidance stick and pressed the throttle as far as it would go. He knew he might pass out from the g-forces, but he had to risk it.

The invisible, brutal hand of g-force shoved Lam deeply into his seat, but he managed to move his hand enough for switching on his viewing screen to see if the Doomen fighters were following yet. To his amazement, instead of Doomen ships hot in pursuit, he saw two bright flashes where the ships had been. Lam reasoned that his eyes were deceiving him as his head swam from the force of the gravity that pulled him and made his flesh ripple.

In the doorway of one of the port hangars, quite pleased with himself, stood Hud, smirking. As he watched the burning debris that had once been Dominion fighters, he shook his head in mock concern and spoke to himself.

"One should always check his engines for fission detonators before taking off."

Chapter Twelve

Exalted Kurdon," invoked the Doomen commander's voice from the viewing screen in Kurdon's flagship.

"Speak, Commander," declared Kurdon from his seat.

"Padeus is on Tsu."

Kurdon's eyebrows raised almost imperceptibly at the news. "How do you know?"

"The planet is in rebellion. We've lost contact with three Doomen. The rest of us have assembled at the space station to exterminate the Palace City when Padeus arrives."

"Really . . ." uttered Kurdon cautiously. "Proceed with the attack, but issue an all-out emergency alert. Prepare for an enemy strike force. We know they have at least one ship and are armed. Based on your soldiers' recent performances, I know it will take more than offensive power to annihilate the Padeus." Then more sternly he added, "That is why we are on our way."

The screen returned to a view of Kurdon's shrinking planet. The Dominion armada had finally departed, but long after Kurdon's deadline. Supply and fueling problems on the destroyer had delayed the mission. Kurdon leaned back on his seat and sat deathlike—except for an occasional slap against his palm with his rod.

"Approaching the light gate," announced Kurdon's communications officer from behind. Nodding his acknowledgment, Kurdon took a deep breath and whispered softly and menacingly, "I will be there soon, Worm King."

The ship began to shimmer and the edges of the equipment and the ship itself became blurred. Kurdon closed his eyes as the entire ship passed through the ring of satellites and de-massed, becoming a long, bright bolt of energy. The rest of the ominous fleet followed, one by one piercing the darkness of space at near light speed.

Although Lam slowed down after seeing that he was not followed, he still hurtled through space almost uncontrolled. He did not attempt an orbit, but decided to fly past where he hoped the Tsuian fighters would be and let them try to catch up. Reaching the dark side of the planet, opposite the space station, Lam exulted at the sight of their waiting wing lights.

"I guess it's that time, folks," Lam announced into his com-link as he flew toward them.

"Lam! Where've you been?" blurted the squadron leader.

"It's a long story," replied Lam, "and one thing we don't have is time. I'm not stopping, so arm your guns and follow me. When you see the Doomen on your screens, mark the one closest to your coordinate and fire. And do it fast—I'm afraid they might be expecting us."

The engines of the fighters flared as they pursued Lam around the planet. Most of the ships had an experienced pilot, a younger co-pilot and gunner. The pilots had flown before the Doomen occupation, but had not flown since then for lack of Dominion pilot's licenses. Their faces were set with concentration. The rest were rookies who now struggled to remember their training and gawked around awestruck by the experience. These novices controlled the top guns that in most cases had a 360° range and could hit anything above the ship. The pilots controlled the belly guns that could shoot only straight ahead.

"If we don't get them on the first pass," Lam's voice crackled in the com-links, "we'll have to get behind them to be safe and then knock them out. If their formation splits, we split too and each team will cover its partner."

The Tsuian fleet, led by Starjumper, left the shadow of Tsu and saw the sun rising from the side of the planet. Its rays spilled over the horizon, bathing the gleaming ships in brightness. The sun made it impossible to see through the viewing port, but Lam's monitor showed what he was watching for, and what he did not want to see.

"Doomen." Lam would not have had to say it. The Tsuians saw them on their viewing screens also. Almost as Lam spoke, the space was laced with red bolts from the Doomen fighters.

"They don't exactly look surprised, Lam," said the squadron leader. The Doomen continued to fly toward them as the Tsuians and Lam approached. The Tsuians returned fire, but in the blink of an eye the Doomen had passed.

"Watch it. They'll probably turn back," called Lam to the fleet. He was right. Passing the Tsuian fighters, the four Doomen fighters turned in pursuit and immediately opened fire."

"Teams!" shouted Lam into the com-link. The squadron leader repeated the command in Tsuian for those who did not know Common. "Watch out for the space station," warned Lam.

The ships scattered. Lam knew this strategy should be successful since they outnumbered the Doomen three to one. Instead of joining a team, Lam maintained a straight course toward the space station. He flew across the path of the Doomen fighters, hoping to attract one so the space station would hesitate shooting. Lam could see in his screen that he had gained a shadow and began rocking his ship to avoid being hit by one of the bolts from the pursuing Doomen fighter.

His charge on the space station was over so quickly Lam did not even have a chance to consider how dangerous his strategy was. He swooped over the space station, loosing a volley of bolts. Without looking to see what he had accomplished, he tumbled Starjumper. It was a tactic he had used before, and it worked again. The pursuing Doomen were momentarily confused and slowed down. Lam quickly took advantage. Starjumper's guidance system gauged the ship's rotation, aimed the guns and pierced the Doomen fighter with a Redlyn bolt.

Lam pulled out of his tumble and watched the Doomen fighter spiralling toward the planet, out of control. He knew it would burn up in the atmosphere. Swinging his ship toward the space station to rejoin the fleet, he was in time to see the space station tear apart from the air escaping through the hole made by Starjumper's guns.

"Tell us what we can do, Lam," called the squadron leader, evenly but forcefully. "You can see all of us from where you are."

"They've discovered your weak spot," noted Lam urgently. "They're flying behind and low. Can't the partners of the ones being chased pull behind and blast the Doomen?"

"They break off and pursue another team when they see us coming," explained the squadron leader.

"We're hit!" shouted a voice in the com-link.

"I saw it," Lam jumped in. "Most of it glanced off."

"Pull out if you have to," ordered the squadron leader.

"It looks like you're playing a waiting game with them," criticized Lam. "I think we need to mix things up. Maintain your courses and I'll head you off. When you see me coming, scatter. That should throw them off. Then don't waste any time—let them have it!"

Lam swung Starjumper toward the planet, using the planet's gravitational pull to pick up speed. Then he pulled up and flew straight into the fray. The Tsuians scattered and the Doomen split up, each picking a fighter, and pursued, shooting wildly. Immediately the space lit up like a comet's tail as ships fired. One Doomen ship became a ball of fire and quickly disintegrated. A Tsuian ship was hit and began to spiral toward the planet.

"Pull up!" yelled Lam. "Thrust into orbit!" The squadron leader yelled similar instructions, but the fighter quickly tumbled from sight and then became a brief glowing spot against the cloud cover. Lam cursed and turned his attention to the two remaining Doomen.

Seizing the moment's hesitation, the Doomen had unexpectedly turned and plunged into a powered dive toward the planet. Lam watched them blankly for a moment.

"The Palace City!" Lam cursed his slow reaction and plunged after them. They had a considerable lead, but he knew Starjumper was faster. Soon the Tsuian fighters were also in pursuit.

"Even if I hit them, it won't do much good at this range," Lam said to himself, reviewing his options. "I have to get closer!"

It was a phenomenal chase. Reentering the atmosphere at free-fall speed, the Doomen fighters had their heat-shielded bellies facing the planet. Lam knew they could not fire at the city from that position, so he had time to close in. But he could not get closer without going nose first into the atmosphere and using his engines. His temperature warnings were already flashing, so he was overriding several safety devices.

Through his side port Lam saw the Tsuian fighters near him, also in pursuit. Especially designed to slice through the atmosphere, their craft even had aerodynamic features, but they were not built for such a powered dive. He could see their tips glowing red, then white. One by one they pulled up and were gliding rather than diving. Soon only one was attempting the descent: the squadron leader.

Lam glanced sideways at his friends, then ahead at his enemies. "Pull up!" Lam yelled into the com-link, but he knew the crew members would never hear above the roar of the dive. Making matters worse, they were entering Tsu's cloud cover and the Doomen fighters had become more difficult to see. The Tsuian ship opened fire on the Doomen fighter in front of it. Lam turned his attention to the chase and also began launching the Redlyn bolts.

"Just a little closer!" Lam screamed, yanking off the com-link clipped to his head and wiping away the sweat. "By the Source and the Power, just a little closer!" Lam called in his desperation.

With the next pull of the activator, the red flash ended in a ball of flame. The Doomen ship was destroyed. A second explosion near it marked the end of the other Doomen fighter. Lam yelled in joy as he pulled up, then activated the gravity resistors.

The Tsuian ship pulled up too, but could not slow down as easily, for it had no gravity resistors. As the fighter glided past Lam, he could see that it had sustained some damage and that parts of the hull had burned away.

"We won't be able to land," announced the squadron leader. "See what you can do about getting us a shuttle or something, okay?"

"Just relax and try not to use up your air," Lam instructed flatly. "It may take some time to launch a shuttle, depending on who's in charge down there." There were too many emotions jumbled up inside him to say much. "The rest of you meet me at the port."

The exhausted space warriors dragged themselves across

the pavement of the port, their still-hot ships warming their backs. It had been a costly victory, and they were too spent to feel like heroes.

Lam's entire body ached. His injured leg was throbbing, his hands stiff from gripping the controls. He was afraid he might have the bends and he was so exhausted he thought he'd collapse. Lam couldn't even remember what it felt like to be rested and comfortable. He leaned heavily on his cane as he walked, wishing he had a second cane now. He observed the wreckage of the Doomen fighters that never took off and the charred guard post. There was no sign of life, giving an eerie appearance of having been that way for ages.

"Listen," called one of the older pilots, holding up his hand. The others stopped and strained to hear. At first the only sound heard was the wind flapping their open flight jackets. Then they all heard it.

"It's cheering coming from the palace!" exclaimed another pilot, pointing his hand. "The King must be here!"

"And do you renounce any allegiance to the Dominion and to Cathra?" demanded King Padeus boldly. He stood in his royal robes on the palace ledge. The palace guard knelt before him while thousands of Tsuians watched from the streets of the city.

The King held the voice-caster to them as they answered, "Yes." Again the crowd cheered.

Padu took back the voice-caster and continued. "And do you swear loyalty to the divinely ordained and commonly established rule of the Council and its elected King, in the name of the Power and the Source?" Again they answered yes, and the King declared, "Praise to the Source and the Power!" The crowd exploded in cheers.

Lam and the pilots had reached the massive crowd and were watching from their large transport suspended just above the heads of the people on the ground. The man kneeling closest to Padu rose from his knees and whispered something to the King. Padu handed him the voice-caster and the man spoke.

"Before these witnesses today, King Padeus, I make my confession. I served as Commander of the Palace Guard under the Royal Council. When Cathra came to power, I resigned my position but I continued in the guard."

The man who spoke, dressed in the simple uniforms the Dominion supplied, was shorter than most of the Tsuians, but also much stockier. It looked strange to see this burly man at the point of tears.

Struggling to finish his speech he cried out, "But I share my comrades' guilt in that we served the Dominion and even guarded against your return. Now we have renounced our former allegiance and sworn faithfulness to you and the Way of Tsu. We could do no other and still keep our lives. However, if you had spared our lives but refused our repentance, I would not consider life worth living; I would join the former commander in death below. I could not bear to face life not in service to the Source and the Power, and the King."

The King embraced him warmly, took back the voice-caster and announced, "I hereby restore you, Haml, to your former position as Commander of the Palace Guard. This people will look to you as friend and guardian from this day on." Again cheers erupted from the masses below.

Padu motioned for Jern to bring Cathra forward to where he stood at the wall. "Is this the man, Cathra, who was appointed governor by the unholy Dominion?" asked Padu through the voice-caster. The crowd shouted that he was.

"Did he rule fairly with the welfare of the people in mind? And did he advance the worship of the Source and the Power?"

"No!" shouted the people.

Lam could not be sure from the distance, but Cathra appeared to be shaking.

Padu continued. "Other serious charges are leveled against you. You imprisoned and wounded members of the movement loyal to the Way of Tsu. You did this through lies and deceit. Finally, you attempted by force to stop my return. Do you have an answer to any of these charges?"

Cathra stood silently with his head bowed.

After a few moments of silence Padu said, "I thought not. For your treason you will die."

Cathra gazed up in shock, his face drained of all color, his eyes filled with hate. The masses below stood spellbound.

Padu continued, "But you will not receive your punishment at our hands; it will come at the hands of the Dominion. Such is the way of those who gain by violence; in the end it takes the life of the violent. I urge you to make your peace with the Source and plead with the Power before that time comes."

"That sounds like the kind of confusing thing Padu would say," Lam muttered quietly with the hint of a smile.

"Good people of Tsu," said the King gravely as Jern led the bound Cathra away, "you know the Doomen. Horrible though they were, they are only shadows cast by the greater evil that approaches. Please understand what I say. We have not yet experienced the wrath of the Dominion, and the Power has revealed to me that we soon will. At this time in our history we have only one chance to survive as a people—to flee this planet we love!"

He paused to let his words take their affect. The people wondered if he really meant what they were sure he had said.

"Believe me, we have won a great victory this day, and though leaving seems a backward blow, we must evacuate. The former underground, which includes many members of the Royal Council, will assist you in your preparations. Those without ships will be taken on a carrier that has been prepared." The people were dumfounded, but they could see that the King was sincere.

"We will return again, but only when it is safe. There is no time to finish your business, to bring in crops, or to visit with loved ones. We *must* flee at once!"

The staggering news came with unforeseeable force. No one moved; no one spoke; no one knew what to think.

Padu's voice once again broke the silence. "I will be instructing the leaders in our next step. Remain here for orders."

Lam and his fellow pilots abandoned their transport. The crowd was too thick to enable them to reach the palace except by pressing through on foot. The pilots found the King in the banquet hall instructing Hud, Melena, Jern, Haml and the other leaders on how to execute the exodus, and how to answer the many questions that would arise. When Padu saw the pilots, he pointed to them and the crowd in the hall greeted them with applause.

"All of you did not return?" questioned the King, peering into their faces.

"Two now wait for us on the Other Side," explained one of the older pilots sadly. "Two more are stranded in orbit. If we had not delayed—"

The King raised his hand to interrupt the pilot's accusation. He then walked to Lam, whose head already hung with guilt. Padu embraced him and turned to address the others.

"Hud and Jern have already informed me of Lam's delaying the space attack by becoming involved in taking the palace. Let everyone be aware that had Lam not led the diversion on the palace and freed the underground prisoners, Hud would not have gone before him to sabotage the port guard and the Doomen fighters. Lam would never have made it to his ship without Hud's help, and the entire mission would have failed. What appeared to be a costly delay was in reality the work of the Source. His sovereignty has covered our arrival and the actions of Lam."

The hushed room gave way to praises of the Source, and many gathered around to embrace Lam. The heavy guilt having been lifted, Lam's emotions nearly gave way.

Padu restored order to the meeting and finished instructing the leaders on the evacuation procedures. Lam sat visibly shaken, but relieved to find he had not failed.

Dismissing the leaders, Padu called Lam aside. His serious expression told Lam something worse was coming than he cared to hear at this point. "There is one more thing," he whispered. "Do you remember the words spoken concerning me on Saan?"

"How could anyone forget them?" Lam managed to say through his constricted throat. *But*, thought Lam, *they had won now, and the King was not killed. He couldn't die.* "But—" protested Lam, angry that Padu would suggest it.

"The Doomen have pursued me these past few years. It is no secret they want me dead. It is time to use that fact to our advantage."

Chapter Thirteen

The leading ships in the Dominion's armada appeared as shimmering outlines in Tsu's light gate. One by one they passed through and re-massed. Kurdon shook his head, clearing his thoughts and glared into his viewing screen. Tsu's bright clouds filled the screen and Kurdon slowly rose to his feet. He walked to the screen and then stared past it to the planet below.

"Carrier commander requesting approach instructions."

"Zenith approach to orbit at 20.43 marks."

"Multiple sub red tracings . . ."

"Debris in course . . ."

Kurdon half listened to the pilot and navigational chatter as he gazed at the image of the planet. He could also see the debris they mentioned—the remains of the space station the Dominion had established to guard the light gate. Several wide beams from the wreckage were still tumbling as his ship passed.

Soon the Dominion armada had entered orbit around Tsu. Kurdon turned to the Doomen who stood by his seat.

"Where do you sense we should direct our attack?" he heartlessly asked the Doomen.

The Doomen stood motionless for a moment and then rasped, "On the planet. Near the port."

Kurdon immediately commanded "Launch the fighters! Bring this ship and the destroyer closer in to the port. When each ship is in range have it fire at will until the city is destroyed."

Kurdon's expression intensified as he listened to his orders being communicated. The Doomen fighters emerged quickly from the carrier like killer insects from a hive and began the descent

98

to the planet. He felt his own ship begin the descent.

"Exalted Kurdon," said his communications officer when the armada was almost in range of the Palace City, "we have determined that a large fleet of ships has recently left the planet. According to the analysis of their tracings, they should be in orbit on the other side of the planet."

Kurdon instantly swung around to face the officer and ordered, "Instruct the Doomen commander to recall the fighters immediately and begin pursuit of those ships. Tell the commander of the Regular Forces to recall the destroyer. It must return to guard the light gate." Kurdon glanced back at the screen, then back at his pilot. In a much calmer voice he said, "Take this ship to the Palace City port. The Doomen cannot be so far wrong— what I want is still down there."

Lam's face was stern and expressionless as he punched buttons and watched the indicators on the control panel. Melena stared blankly through one of the viewing ports on Starjumper, watching the unblinking stars stare back at her.

Hud observed his downcast companions and addressed them gently, "It was hard for me, too. We said goodbye to him fifteen years ago, believing we would be together again one day. Now it seemed we barely had greeted him when we had to say goodbye again."

Lam continued to stare at his instruments. His voice betraying anger, and grief, he said, "Yeah, well, I never understood what he was doing; and I sure don't this time. Why did he give up without a fight?" No one spoke and the silence was unbearable. Lam decided to change the subject. "We were lucky to fit everyone in a ship. It's a good thing you had the carrier."

"We never planned on using it for this, that's for sure," replied Hud. "But I know there are some who did not come."

"It's hard to leave everything you've worked for all your life," noted Lam sympathetically. "Especially when you're not sure why."

"Well, one thing is certain," said Hud, "it wasn't easy getting this evacuation organized in a few days."

Lam thought back to those frantic days of preparation. Provisions were stocked. People were shuttled to the carrier. Records were made. Yet somehow Padu managed to find a few moments to talk to Lam.

"Do you know," Padu had asked in the quiet privacy of one of the palace chambers, "that chance does not rule in the lives of those who follow the Source and the Power?" Lam's puzzled expression told Padu to simplify it. "What I am saying is that it was no accident we met on Saan. I know you are not at all comfortable with us or even yourself now, but I know that will change." As Lam wondered what Padu was getting at, Padu removed the chain and amulet from around his neck and dropped it into Lam's lap. "I will no longer need this. It is not a symbol of authority nor a magical charm; it is a symbol of the Power and an expression of our faith. When you feel the time is right, you may wear it."

Lam did not know what to say. He wasn't even sure if "Thank you" was a proper response. He simply stared at the softly glowing stone in his lap while Padu stood, embraced him and returned to the evacuation preparations. Now, as Lam guided the Tsuian fleet, he felt the firmness of the amulet in his pocket and wished Padu were here to explain all that he had said.

It was an unsightly fleet he led: old supply vessels, shuttles, and other assorted craft—anything with an Emec. The Tsuian fighters flanked the convoy and covered the rear. Lam, Melena, Hud, and Maxai were in Starjumper at the head.

"We're getting close to the light gate," said Lam.

"What is it like where we are going?" asked Melena. Those were the first words she had spoken since they left the planet. Now it seemed she was looking ahead.

"It's a system with a pair of type-two planets and a type-one planet," explained Lam, "besides all the normal rocks and meteors."

"You called the type-one planet 'Refuge,' but I've never heard of it."

"Well," Lam said, hesitating, "it's been charted for a long time, but never colonized because very few people know it has a light gate."

"Who put the light gate there?" she asked. Lam's face tightened again, so she knew it was not an open subject. "What is Refuge like?"

"Beautiful," he informed her, relaxing. "It's like your planet in some ways, but it has several continents and is much more, well, wild. There is no intelligent life we know of, but it's blanketed with forests."

Lam glanced at Melena sitting beside him. She nodded that she had heard, then smiled. But her sorrow-filled eyes were distant as she stared out the viewing port.

Lam sighed and thought about Refuge. He had been there only twice. The pirate cartel used it as a place of escape when pursued. They also used it to relax on occasion, knowing they would be safe from the Dominion. He wished he was already on the lakeshore, breathing the fresh air, his face to the blue sky.

He was shaken from his daydreams by an alarm chirping from his control panel. A green grid pattern superimposed his viewing screen, and a flashing green square marked the light gate.

"Settle in," Lam announced, "we're nearing the light gate. Everybody strapped in?"

Starjumper would be passing through first, so Lam leaned back and got comfortable. Another alarm sounded and Lam jumped forward in his seat and stared at the viewing screen. Moving the field around for a better look, he saw the last thing he expected—or wanted.

"Doomen fighters!"

Their red bolts flashed in the ports. His com-link was filled with pilots begging for instructions. Lam counted at least twenty fighters rising on the planet's horizon. They were still too distant to be very accurate or dangerous, but they were closing in. Then his screen showed a blip coming from the other side of the planet. He turned the viewing screen to visual, then gasped and slumped into his chair. Hud and Melena unbuckled and leaned over to see.

"A destroyer," uttered Hud after a deep breath.

Lam seemed to recover, then spoke calmly into the com-link, "We are under attack. Fighters return fire, but do not break formation—we're almost to the light gate." Lam's commands were clear and urgent. The Tsuians launched their own red bolts at the approaching Dominion armada.

"We won't last a moment if that destroyer gets in range," whispered Lam harshly to Hud and Melena.

A beam erupted from the destroyer and struck Starjumper and the two ships behind her. The lights in the cabin blinked momentarily, alarms sounded and indicators went wild.

"We're still all right," Lam assured his passengers. As he spoke the ship's interior began to shimmer. Lam saw lights begin to flash in his eyes, and his ears began to ring. He could still see the action in the viewing screen. Melena inhaled sharply as the Doomen fleet launched another volley of Redlyn bolts. The fighters had been closing in behind them rapidly and were dangerously close. One of the bolts scored a direct hit on the tail of a Tsuian fighter. Lam saw the fighter's wing rip off and fuel spray out. The ship started tumbling away from the fleet.

That's Jern and Wil! he thought, but he could not speak. Starjumper became a flash of light and was gone. The other ships followed her one by one like lightning strikes.

"Cease fire!" ordered the commander of the Regular Forces as he stood on the bridge of the destroyer. He turned to the Doomen commander beside him and cautioned sharply, "If your Doomen keep shooting, they'll destroy the light gate and we'll be stranded here."

On the planet below, Kurdon's menacing flagship landed on the flowered ground cover of the palace courtyard. The port hissed open and the ramp descended. Kurdon walked slowly and deliberately down the ramp. He was followed by an armed soldier and a Doomen, each surveying the courtyard and watching for danger. Scurvit hung back at the port and then hurried after them when they reached the lawn.

Kurdon slapped his rod against his hand, gazed about and waited. The breeze tousled his hair, but the wind was the only sound heard—even the birds seemed to have fled. Scurvit became very apprehensive as he stood behind the guards; Kurdon simply stood and waited.

Finally, a figure appeared in the brown stone archway leading to the palace. The guards immediately raised their shoulder blasters and aimed. Kurdon held his hand up to stop them. Then he took a few steps and stopped again. The figure in the arch began to approach. It was Padu. His royal robes billowed behind him as he strode to meet Kurdon. Soon the two men faced each other. Kurdon and Padu were the same height, although Kurdon looked as if he could have picked up Padu and cast him aside with one arm. Neither spoke for several moments.

Kurdon grinned maliciously and hissed, "You are the troublemaker I came so far to face?"

Padu smiled and nodded. His face reflected a tranquillity that somewhat unnerved Kurdon. But Kurdon knew he was in control. The Worm King was in his hands.

"I would invite you to my ship for a drink, but I can't trust you," alleged Kurdon menacingly, the red stones in his breastplate beginning to glow more intensely. "I intend to end our adversary relationship here and now."

Padu said nothing, but unpredictably slipped off his robe. He stood in the same traveling clothes he wore when he first met Lam on Saan. Kurdon's guards stiffened and again prepared to shoot, but then saw he had no weapons. Padu spread open his arms and apparently welcomed Kurdon's aggression. Kurdon glared at Padu and could see that the King was no longer looking at him but past him, with a distant expression. Kurdon was infuriated that Padu did not even seem to care what was happening to him. The King even betrayed a hint of a smile, as if waiting to greet a friend.

Kurdon burst into incredible profanity and held out his metal rod which began to glow red as his stones did. He swung and the rod sang through the air just before it cut into Padu's body. Padu groaned as it bit into him, then slumped to the ground, staining the flowers with his blood. He had won his final victory over Kurdon: gaining precious moments for the fleet by drawing Kurdon to the planet. He had stared his enemy in the eye and declared that Padu himself served the greater Master. Death held no terror to Padu.

Looking down at his handiwork, Kurdon could not believe that it was over. It had seemed too easy.

"What now?" whispered Cathra to himself. He had been forced to stay behind, guarded by Padu. Cowering behind a column in the archway he had witnessed the murder. He had seen Padu meet Kurdon; he had seen Padu fall. Now he watched Kurdon sweep with his hand, ordering his Doomen guard to search the palace.

"He's coming this way," whispered Cathra, clutching the column with white knuckles. "How could I have served these horrible people? Should I surrender? After all, I served them faithfully—but I failed."

Finally his own fear decided for him. As the Doomen approached, Cathra turned and dashed for the archway that led to the palace. Sensing him immediately, the Doomen raised his shoulder blaster and unleashed a red bolt that tore into the stone work of the archway. Much of it crumbled and fell to the ground. Cathra fell and attempted to scramble across the loose stone as he choked on the dust.

"No, no!" he shouted. "I'm one of you!" The Doomen aimed again. A high-pitched whine sounded from his shoulder blaster and another red bolt ripped through the air and slammed Cathra against the stones. In anguish he looked up to the sky and mouthed the words, "I'm sorry. . . ," then collapsed. The Doomen walked to where he lay and kicked the lifeless body to make sure Cathra was dead.

"Exalted Kurdon," conveyed Scurvit to his master, "your communications officer reports that the Tsuian fleet, except for one fighter, has escaped through the light gate."

Kurdon stood motionless on the field of battle. Having just destroyed his greatest enemy, any sense of personal victory had been short-lived. He had played the fool and lost. Kurdon spoke in a trembling, barely controlled voice. "Do we know their destination?"

"We have intercepted their transmissions," answered Scurvit, "but we do not know their navigational codes. We hope to learn more from the captured ship's programming." He attempted to sound positive, though he held little hope of finding it.

"Instruct our communications technicians to begin work on

this immediately," commanded Kurdon sharply, taking charge again. Then in a more menacing tone, "And instruct the Doomen commander to place the commander of the Regular Forces under arrest. I warned him that we could not afford a delay in reaching Tsu."

Scurvit bowed and ran up the ramp. Kurdon scanned the two bodies before him, and at the palace. Again the eerie quiet of the city gripped him.

Kurdon paused over Padu's body and breathed menacingly, "I will find them."

Again Scurvit hurried down the ramp with a message. "Exalted Kurdon," he appealed bowing, "the Doomen commander requests your wishes for this planet."

"Level the cities, but leave the countryside. We will make sure that any survivors are put to work raising food for the Dominion."

Chapter Fourteen

Starjumper to all ships," said Lam into his com-link after re-massing at the Refuge gate. He felt strange to be suddenly safe. He watched the ships materialize in the gate one by one. "Starjumper to all ships, someone didn't make it—what happened at the light gate?"

"Starjumper, this is Nova. The last fighter was hit by a Doomen—they never reached the light gate."

Lam's face was grave; he sat quietly for a moment as the news sunk in. "Thank you, Nova," he finally said sadly. He turned to Melena and Hud. It was hard for Lam to tell what they were feeling, but he could imagine. He had lost loved ones before.

"I don't think they're dead," Melena announced quietly. "But I believe my father is."

"What do you mean?" Lam asked.

A frown creased her otherwise smooth forehead. Her dark eyes seemed a little shinier than usual. "Well, it's just something we can sense," she related. Lam did not understand her any better than he had Padu. Instead, he turned to the control panel and spoke harshly into his com-link.

"Starjumper to all ships, prepare to receive instructions." Then he remembered his companions and his tone softened. "You know that I haven't been here in many years—I don't know what it's like now. I'll give instructions for the carrier and most of the ships to orbit while we and a couple of fighters land and see what preparations have to be made before the others land. They have provisions for a couple of days, so it should be all right."

"Ouch!" exclaimed Maxai, jerking in his seat. Lam was not expecting such a reaction to his announcement. Maxai frantically reached into his pocket and yanked out the small bag of M-stones he had carried when posing as a trader. He held it by the draw string because of the heat the stones were throwing off. He sighed and relaxed. An intense blue-white light glowed from the bag, so bright that it pierced the weave of the heavy fabric.

"Do they do that often?" asked Lam.

"I've never seen it before!" exclaimed Maxai.

"There must be a vast deposit of the stone on this planet," asserted Hud, raising his eyebrows. "And these stones have always been a symbol of the guidance of the Power."

Far removed from the peace of Refuge, Kurdon stood in the detention center of the Dominion destroyer. The commander of the Regular Forces stood in his cell, at attention and proud. He knew he had served well and had done everything possible to ensure the success of their mission. Kurdon, however, did not see it that way. He nodded at the Doomen beside him.

The Doomen raised his Redlyn pistol to the level of the commander's chest and fired point blank. The commander's face twisted with agony and anger as he fell against the back of the cell and slumped to the floor.

"Dispose of him," Kurdon told the two young crew members that stood outside the cell. They switched off the energy bars and entered the cell to retrieve the body.

Kurdon turned to the Doomen and said, "Your commander will assume command of the fleet until a replacement is made." The Doomen nodded.

"Exalted Kurdon," puffed Scurvit as he approached, "the fighters are returning from Tsu. They have finished."

In the busy space above Tsu, the wreck of Wil and Jern's fighter floated, bathed in the harsh light of the sun. The light glinted jaggedly from the torn metal as the craft tumbled slowly in a decaying orbit. A shadow engulfed the ship which was soon dwarfed by the approaching Dominion destroyer. Two shuttles emerged from what seemed a tiny opening in the belly of the great ship. They sped toward the helpless wreck and flanked it.

Molten metal sprayed from nozzles on the shuttles and spun a net, solidifying in the cold of space, which enwrapped the wreck between the vehicles. Thus secured, they towed the ship to the destroyer where they were swallowed.

Inside, miraculously, Jern and Wil were alive, wearing pressure suits to protect themselves from the rip in their hull. They spoke by pressing their helmets together rather than risking detection by using com-links.

"So what do you think?" yelled Jern. Wil's answer was faint, although he too was shouting.

"I've been captured by better outfits than this!"

"I'd laugh if we weren't wrapped up like a fish in the stomach of a Dominion destroyer," Jern replied.

"You know," called Wil in a more serious tone, "there's not much we can do against an entire army. They'll take the demassing instructions from the Emec and find out exactly where the fleet went."

"Or," suggested Jern grimly, "they'll interrogate us for the information and then kill us."

In silence they came to the same conclusion. Using manual controls they began to flood the engines with fuel and arm the cannons.

The docking bay doors closed behind the tiny fighter as jaws around a morsel. The craft was secured magnetically to the floor of a small pressurized bay dock. Two bay workers with cutting torches and two technicians with Emec deprogrammers surrounded the apparently lifeless vessel. The bay workers ignited their torches and approached the fighter.

Chapter Fifteen

Do you see that flashing green dot?" Lam asked Hud who was seated next to him. Hud gazed at the light on the viewing screen. As Starjumper broke through the clouds, Hud could see the landscape clearly in the viewing screen. The flashing green dot was on the edge of a glistening lake.

"There should be a large sandy beach there," continued Lam. "The beacon was left there to help locate the beach." Padu had warned Hud not to ask Lam too many questions, so he resisted asking who left the beacon there. Starjumper's passengers gripped their seats as Lam landed the ship in the sand.

"Sorry it was a little rough," said Lam, eager to get out of the ship. "I'm too used to automated landings, I guess." Hud, Melena and Maxai were still unbuckling and getting out of their seats while Lam was already up and opening the port. It hissed open and Lam, with a bow, said, "Welcome to Refuge."

"Thank you," replied Melena. She grabbed the handrail and was about to step down when Lam shouted, "Wait!"

"Remember, this is a wild planet. I'm not sure what we'll find. Have these ready," Lam pronounced, holding up his Redlyn pistol. They complied and stepped one by one onto the sand. Lam was last, hurrying down the steps, wishing his leg would let him jump to the ground. When he joined the group, the others were busy absorbing their surroundings.

"It's beautiful!" exclaimed Melena, somewhat awed. "It's so thick with vegetation—and those wild flowers are so delicate!"

Lam was staring at the lake. It was every bit as beautiful as he remembered, and always his favorite feature of the scenery. Its blue expanse held so much peace; its surface rippled only occasionally from a gentle breeze or a floating water bird. At those times the lake appeared as though a handful of shining gem stones had been hurled across the water as the bright sun sparkled on the rippled surface.

Lam would have loved to stay there all day, but they had another mission before them. He turned and said to Melena, "Maybe you and Hud should stay with the ship and meet the fighters when they land. Maxai and I can go to survey how much beach we have available for landing. We'll also check a bunker that's nearby; it should hold some things we'll need, at least the immunizations."

"If you're going to be gone long, be sure to check in with us," warned Melena. Lam smiled at her concern and struck off down the beach while Melena watched. Except for a few small animal tracks, the men's footprints were the only ones in the sand.

"It's terribly overgrown," called Lam as they approached the solid block bunker. Vines covered it, making it difficult to spot. "And not just the bunker either . . ." Lam motioned with his hand to the edge of the woods. "The sand used to extend much further inland. There was room for about seven ships the size of Starjumper, but now this is all brush." He squinted into the brush and stared at a glint that shone between the branches.

"Is that a ship back there? Let's get to the bunker first and then we'll check out this landing area." Lam lifted his pistol and loosed a bolt as he moved his arm in a sweeping motion. Several saplings fell partway but were caught by vines that seemed to tie them all together. "What a mess."

Lam and Maxai trampled their way through the brush to the bunker. Lam pressed a catch on the handle of his pistol and a short blade snapped out. He began pulling on the vines and leaning into them with his blade. Maxai pulled away the vines Lam had already cut.

"I think we've found the door," said Lam, continuing his struggle with the vines. He banged his hand on the door and he could hear the metallic echo inside the bunker. "There's no latch," said Lam stepping back. He jumped forward and slammed his shoulder against the door. It groaned slightly. Maxai joined his second attempt, and it grated open enough for them to squeeze through. A sour mustiness repelled them for a moment. Lam then reached and slapped the wall where he knew a light switch should be. The switch snapped and light flooded the bunker.

"What in the galaxy?" cried Lam, startled. The light had illuminated not only the dusty shelves and cannisters, but a skeleton, lying on a low cot, draped with tatters of cloth. The intruders approached the cot. Their boots echoed loudly on the concrete floor in the otherwise silent room.

Lam picked up a pistol that rested near the remains and snapped open the pistol's rod compartment.

"It's got a spent Redlyn rod." He laid the weapon down and looked again at the body.

"I wonder how he died," said Maxai reverently.

"It's hard to say," answered Lam looking around. "But it appears all the food stores and water supplies are gone. He must have been stranded here. Probably starved to death."

They pulled a dusty blanket over the skeleton and examined the bunker. Empty cans and kegs littered the floor, sharing space with five chairs, a table, and three cots. Shelves and cabinets lined the walls. Between the cabinets on one wall hung some tools. Lam pulled down a large curved blade and handed it to Maxai.

He took one himself and suggested, "We can use these to start clearing brush away from the landing area." Then he stepped to a cabinet and opened it; dust cascaded from the top of the door. Lam scrutinized the first aid supplies and other medical equipment.

"It looks as if most of it's used up," noted Maxai. Lam coughed and agreed.

"I don't know what's been going on here," said Lam. "It's never been this bad before. As least there's plenty of the immunization left. It protects against the major bacteria and viruses found on this planet."

"Well," began Maxai, "it's good to have, but we don't get sick very often."

"I don't know, Max," Lam cautioned. "You'd better all take it as a precaution, although someone should try it first." At that

Maxai rolled up his sleeve and held out his arm. Lam took out one of the disposable vials and attached it to the inoculator. He held it to Maxai's arm and it was over with a click.

"Let's go find the landing pad," called Lam, squeezing through the door. Maxai followed and they began hacking at brush.

"You seem pretty energetic," said Maxai, panting from the exertion. Lam swung hard at a large bush with black berries that splattered on him as he cut.

"I guess I just like this place," declared Lam swinging.

Max took a break to lean on his blade and mumbled, "Well, I'm not sure I like it here. I don't mind the work, although my arms are already getting sore, but I'm not used to seeing skeletons lying around."

"I have to admit," uttered Lam between his teeth as he yanked on the bush to pull its roots out of the sand, "that skeleton makes me a little nervous. But at least there are no Doomen around."

"I think that bush needs more than a few yanks," said Maxai drawing his pistol. Lam stood back and Maxai aimed at the bush and released a bolt. It hit the sand and melted a spot into a glob of glass.

"You missed," laughed Lam uncontrollably. Maxai shot a glance at Lam that said "I know," and pointed again.

"Wha—?" shouted Maxai as a vine wrapped itself around his arm. He jerked to see Lam crash onto the sticks they had been standing on. Maxai saw that vines weighted with stones had been thrown and wrapped around Lam's legs and his own pistol. Another vine swung around Maxai's legs and he went down with a thud.

Lam's head was reeling from the fall and the surprise. He heard sounds like howling from the woods around him; then he felt hands grab his feet and arms. Lying face down, he struggled to turn his head and saw sinewy legs covered with gray and brown fur, ending in feet with a row of claws. The creatures swiftly tied Lam's hands behind his back and yanked him roughly into the woods. Lam yelled angrily as his face dragged on the ground, his broken curses drowning out the angry calls of disturbed birds.

"What are you? Let us go!" Lam yelled. He heard Maxai somewhere behind him, groaning with each scrape and bruise. The creatures pulled him quickly into the thicker, darker interior of the woods. Lam tried to roll to one side so he could see what was happening, but cracked his head on a protruding rock. He winced and saw stars. A moment later everything went black.

When the destroyer's bay workers pried open the Tsuian fighter's hatch, they found themselves facing readied pistols. Not even the Doomen commander dreamed anyone could have survived in the broken ship. Jern ripped off his helmet and whispered harshly in Tsuian, "Don't move or say a word." He trusted that they understood. Three of them were too stunned to move anyway. One of the bay workers ran at them with a lit torch, but Jern shot him in the foot.

Wil took off his helmet and asked, "Now what should we do with them?"

"Don't ask me, you're the royal one around here."

"Well," deliberated Wil considering their options, "I suppose we could tie them up and take their uniforms." They forced the two technicians into the fighter, tied them with their own belts, and secured gags over their faces.

"I don't think either of their uniforms will fit you let alone me," said Wil looking at their captives. Jern had just finished lashing the last of the dock workers to the fighter's landing struts. "Let's just finish getting this thing ready to blow and then try to find transportation out of here."

The dock they were standing in was small and had room enough only for their fighter. Large doors led to the bay.

"Do you think these smaller doors lead to another dock, or do they lead to the interior of the ship?" asked Jern as Wil finished sabotaging the remains of their fighter.

"How should I know," sighed Wil in an annoyed tone.

"I'll go see," Jern said, running toward the doors.

"Wait a minute! You need someone to cover you," said Wil, as he crossed a final wire and then pulled out the programming card for the Emec that contained the de-massing instructions for travel to Refuge.

He looked at their captives and said in Tsuian, "Be sure to tell your commander that if anyone starts touching these controls, the ship will explode." The men did not respond except to glare back at him. Wil jumped down and ran to where Jern had opened the portal and was looking down the passageway.

"It looks safe," Jern stated. Wil did not think "safe" was quite the right word, but he stuffed the programming card into his boot and followed Jern into the passageway.

They made slow progress, peering around corners and ducking into nooks whenever they heard footsteps. Reaching a door they thought might be large enough to lead to a bay, they raised pistols and prepared to shoot their way through to a ship. Jern drew a breath and pressed the door opener. The door hissed open and the Tsuians leaped into the room. It was not a bay. It was a storage closet.

"For some reason I can't help but think we'll be on the Other Side before we escape this destroyer."

"I'm ready either way," answered Wil in a more serious tone. Jern nodded that he was too, and they paused to survey the room.

"Servoids," groaned Jern in a discouraged murmur, looking at the rows of knee-high robots that lined the walls.

"But look at this, Jern," observed Wil, pointing to long racks of Redlyn pistols in the corner.

Jern replied dryly, "If we had an army to use them we probably could take over the ship." At his joke, Wil's eyes lit up.

"We do have an army!" exclaimed Wil, pointing to the servoids. "Don't you think we can disable their programming so we can control them with remotes alone?"

"I don't think that should be hard if they're already wired for it," Jern answered, pressing the door shut and opening the control panel of the closest servoid.

Soon they had twenty servoids under their control, responding, more or less, to two remotes. Neither of the men had much experience directing robots, especially ten at a time; nevertheless, they placed pistols in each of the mechanical grippers that extended from the top of the servoids.

"I'll go scout ahead," volunteered Jern. He slipped out the

door with his pistol raised. Wil looked over their little army and practiced with the remotes. He could move the servoids forward and back and close their grippers; no more. He hoped it would be enough.

"How did I ever think this could work?" he asked his troops. He did not have enough time to change his mind about their plan before Jern was back.

"I've found the lift to the bridge," Jern announced gleefully. "Let's move out!"

Wil and Jern headed down the passageway to the lift, twenty little servoids rolling behind with pistols raised high, threatening to vaporize anyone who got in their way. Somehow they managed to progress undetected down the passageway and squeezed into the lift. As it sped up to the bridge, their stomachs sank partly from the g-force, and partly in anticipation of their insane attempt for control of the destroyer. Jern studied his partner and saw the same worried concentration on his face.

"It wouldn't have been any easier to steal a ship and get out," Jern defended.

"I know."

"I hope you're praying," said Jern, almost amused, as the indicator showed they were nearing the top of the destroyer.

"I haven't stopped since we left Tsu," Wil answered after forcing a deep breath.

The humming of the lift began to lower in pitch and their stomachs became lighter. Finally the light next to the tag, which read COMMAND CENTER in Common lit up. The lift stopped and the doors opened with a hiss.

The Tsuians jumped out, surprising the guards and grabbing their pistols from them. Others in the command center rushed toward them, reaching for their own weapons.

"Stop!" yelled Jern and Wil in heavily-accented Common. The Dominion crew braked themselves and gaped as the squat metal army rolled out onto the bridge.

The command center was a large triangular area stepped in several levels. Viewing screens and indicators lined the walls. Only blinking lights and electronic voices disturbed the quiet that dominated the center as each occupant waited to see what would happen. All appeared to not believe what they were seeing. Some of the personnel were dressed in loose uniforms and carried recorders and small electronic devices. Others had black padded armor on their shoulders, chest and joints. These stood with their pistols trained on Wil and Jern.

"Put down your weapons!" ordered Wil. No one moved. The Doomen commander drew his pistol and walked slowly to where the Tsuians stood. Wil and Jern nodded to each other and the servoids began shooting. They seemed to have gone wild, spinning and sending continuous red bolts everywhere. The red bolts exploded against the destroyer's control panels, smashing lights. Everyone in the center dropped to the deck, including Wil and Jern who grimaced at their lack of control over their troops. When the fireworks finally stopped, Wil and Jern looked up at the now submissive crew. The Doomen commander was nowhere to be seen.

"Now what?" asked Jern.

Wil stood up and called out, shaking, "Uh, I claim this ship in the name of the Source and the Power!"

"That sounded good," whispered Jern, nudging his partner in the ribs with his elbow. Then he yelled, "Oh no!"

On the other side of the bridge, lift doors flew open and Doomen swarmed into the center, shoulder blasters raised. Wil and Jern, firing furiously at the Doomen, stumbled back into the lift they had arrived in.

"Hit the button!" shouted Jern as he squatted on the lift floor and fired. Bolts laced the air and sparks flew from the metal of the lift as they hit. Several of Jern's bolts slammed into Doomen and toppled them. It was easy to hit one because there were so many, and more were coming, running over the fallen Doomen.

The lift doors slid shut and the Tsuians slid to the floor, leaning against the back of the lift as they panted heavily.

"Plan B?" asked Jern between gasps. Wil nodded his head, his dark hair matted down with sweat. They struggled to their feet and poised to jump out of the lift when it stopped. They readied their pistols and braced themselves as the doors slid open.

"Oh no," said Jern with a groan. As the doors opened, the pair faced two rows of soldiers, waiting for them with shoulder blasters raised. The Tsuians shook their heads and surrendered their weapons. One soldier ran into the lift to pick up their weapons, while two others entered and yanked Jern and Wil out.

"It was fun while it lasted," Jern remarked to Wil as they were marched down the passageway.

The guard behind Jern rapped him in the head with his shoulder blaster and barked, "Silence!"

The soldiers herded them to the detention center; there they stood quietly as the guards discussed with the soldiers where the prisoners should be put. The guards stopped talking as a low rumbling echoed through the ship. They listened. The ship lurched a little and a couple of guards stumbled. As the rumbling persisted alarms began to sound. Jern flashed a crooked smile at Wil.

"Didn't you tell them not to mess with our ship?" Jern asked. Wil gave Jern an uneasy laugh that said he was not happy that they had to do it, but was glad it had worked. The guards shoved them roughly into a cell and activated its ener-bars.

Chapter Sixteen

He liked being a soldier. He hated the Dominion. Kalen Carnes rubbed a polishing cloth across his Redlyn pistol and mused about his life. He rubbed harder as he mourned over the news his friend had brought. The words still pounded in his head: "They executed your father." Kalen inspected his shiny weapon and then threw it across the room. His father was the best commander the Dominion forces had ever had! Kurdon had killed him because of some senseless obsession.

His father had been trapped into joining the Dominion forces—Kalen was sure of it. And when a boy graduates from martial training, he follows in his father's footsteps. Kalen now wished with all his soul that he could have followed his father's footsteps in service to someone besides the butcher Kurdon.

"I promised you, Father . . ." declared Kalen under his breath.

The young man rose from his bunk, retrieved his pistol, tucked it in its holster and slipped out of his cabin into the destroyer's passageway. He walked quickly but cautiously, wanting to be seen by as few people as possible as he approached the room where Kurdon held his audiences. Kalen drew his pistol and his breath. *Good, the portal is closed*, he thought to himself. He slipped past it and paused. He had not been detected. He continued down the hallway.

Kalen stopped at another portal. It bore numerous warnings printed in red. He glanced in both directions, then slipped into the room, looked around until he was satisfied he was alone, then took inventory. The walls were lined with weapons and ammunition. Half of the room stored obsolete munitions. Kalen

118

reached into his tunic and retrieved a small electronic device, a transmitter-controlled detonator tuned to his personal frequency. Kalen ran his hand across the many weapons until he came to the fusion grenades. Picking one up, he glanced around again to be sure he was alone, then fastened the detonator to the grenade. He hurried to the other side of the room and placed the device beneath one of the old warheads. Returning to the grenades, he snatched two off the shelf to hide in his tunic, and returned to the passageway.

Kalen's next stop was the detention area. This time his gait displayed more confidence. He had to give the appearance of having business there.

"I would like to speak to the prisoners alone," said Kalen to the guard in the detention area.

"Yes, sir," the guard replied, and left the area for a brief break. Kalen scrutinized the prisoners a long time before he spoke.

Wil stared back at the young officer who stood outside his cell and wondered what he wanted. Wil noticed the man's hair was only partially tamed, and even his eyes had a wild look in them.

"You caused us a great deal of trouble," said Kalen to the Tsuians.

"What do you want?" demanded Jern, getting off the cot and stalking to the cell opening. Kalen stole a glance around the detention area to make sure they were alone, then spoke quietly.

"My name is Kalen. My father was commander of the Dominion's Regular Forces before—before Kurdon executed him."

Wil and Jern looked at each other but did not know how to respond. They both wondered if this was Kurdon's play to get them to talk.

"I don't expect your sympathy; we are enemies. But I propose an alliance. To show you I mean business, please take this." Kalen carefully guided a small metal rod, about half the length of his finger, through the ener-bars. Wil took it and examined it while Kalen explained, "It is a key that will get you into any of the bays and will unlock the panel of any Dominion ship." Jern whistled softly at hearing how valuable their treasure was.

"What good does it do us in here?" asked Wil skeptically.

"Take this also." Kalen guided a card through the ener-bars. "This contains the Emec instructions for the light gate at the Dominion's home base planet. And one more thing—" Kalen carefully removed a grenade from his tunic and passed it to Wil who recognized it immediately and hid it in his pocket. "You will be taken out of your cell sometime soon for interrogation by Kurdon and the Doomen commander. They will be taking you near the bay area. Make your move then. It will be your last chance because Kurdon will kill you, as he did my father. You have cost him dearly."

Before Wil and Jern could say anything, Kalen turned on his heels and strode from the area, telling the guard to return.

Stepping into the passageway to return to his cabin, Kalen was met by his uniformed friend who had broken to him the news of his father's death. His friend's young face was grave, and he held a pistol which was pointed toward the deck.

"What's the matter?" asked Kalen.

"I really hate to do this Kalen; in fact, it stinks. But I have to—"

"What?" asked Kalen, anxiously.

"I have to arrest you. I've been ordered to."

"Why? What have I done?"

"You are your father's son," pronounced his friend, shrugging his shoulders. "I'll do everything I can to clear you, but for now you'll have to step back into detention with me."

"Don't you want to search me?" asked Kalen bitingly.

"Don't insult me," replied his friend angrily. "Just come and, as I said, I'll do what I can." Kalen went with his friend back into the detention area and this time entered a cell and sat down as the ener-bars hummed to warn they were activated.

Kalen's friend turned to the guard. "Bind the Tsuians and bring them to Kurdon. These guys are in for it!"

"Detention requesting assistance in transferring prisoners," addressed the guard into the com-link. Soon eight armed soldiers were standing by the Tsuians' cell. The guard deactivated the door, bound their hands in front of them and motioned at the soldiers to take them away. As they exited, they passed Kalen's cell. Wil and Jern looked at him, but he did not even look up as they passed.

In the corridors their footsteps echoed loudly, sounding like a small army marching. Wil's nostrils flared as he smelled burnt wiring and he looked at Jern. Jern nodded. They were passing the bay. They ached for an opportunity to escape, but with eight guards and their hands tied, it did not seem likely. Then it happened.

"Fire!" shouted a voice from behind one of the bay doors.

"I thought they took care of them all," cursed one of the soldiers. The bay door opened and a coughing dock worker staggered out.

"The fire has re-ignited in there," stammered the burly man between coughs. All but one of the soldiers ran into the bay to help with the fire. Thick smoke began to billow out. Wil turned the upper half of his body around and glanced past the lone soldier guarding them. He put a shocked expression on his face and shouted in Common, just as the dock worker had done—"Fire!"

When the soldier snapped his head around to see the non-existent fire, Jern leaped up and planted his boot on the side of the soldier's head, sending him sprawling. His shoulder blaster skidded across the floor. Jern picked himself up as Wil pulled the grenade from his tunic. It was somewhat awkward with his hands tied, but he armed it and rolled it into the dock where the soldiers struggled to put out the fire.

"That should really keep them busy," Wil laughed.

"Run!" warned Jern, knowing they did not have much time before the grenade would detonate. They sidestepped the fallen soldier and ran down the hall. The grenade roared and shook the floor. The force of the blast threw the men on their faces. Pieces of metal sang past above their heads and they grimaced from the pain of the noise as they struggled back to their feet.

"The key!" Jern urged. Wil pulled it out of his pocket and fumbled to place it in the lock. His hands shook so hard that it took all his concentration to steady it enough to slide the slender rod into the lock. The door slid open and they ran in. The door sliding shut behind them, they found themselves alone in a dimly lit dock.

"It looks deserted," breathed Jern.

"Good," sighed Wil. "Let's try to keep it that way. What ship is in here anyway?"

As their eyes quickly adjusted to the light, they could see the craft which was docked there.

"A Doomen fighter?" spoke Jern in disbelief.

"You might know it would be," grumbled Wil. "But it beats floating through space in a pressure suit."

The two ran to the craft and found the hatch shut.

"Use the key!" Jern pushed. Wil took the key in his bound hands and fumbled to jam it into a small hole near the hatch. It hissed open.

"Great!" shouted Jern as he scrambled up into the ship. Wil followed and they threw themselves into the seats. The hatch shut behind them.

"How do you start this thing?" asked Wil anxiously, shaking his head and running his hands across the controls.

"We'd better learn fast," urged Jern, "Doomen!" As he spoke, Redlyn bolts screamed against the hull of the fighter. "Those pistols won't damage this thing, but there are plenty of weapons on this destroyer that can."

"I know," uttered Wil as he pulled a lever. His action resulted in a whine as indicator lights flashed to life. "Ha!" exclaimed Wil.

Without waiting for Jern's concurrence, he pulled what obviously were the fighter's gun triggers and red bolts erupted and shattered the dock doors that led to the bay. The air started rushing through the gash, but it did not stop the Doomen.

Jern peered out the small viewing port and yelled, "They've got plasma cannons!"

"Power be with us!" gasped Wil. "Now, hold on!"

He pulled on hand controls and the fighter's engines ignited. The ship pulled against its floor restraint for a moment. Backing away from the exhaust, the Doomen aimed their cannons again. With an incredible crack the restraints broke and the fighter exploded from the dock into the bay. They spun as they entered the bay.

"There are no instructions on these controls!" shouted Wil. Jern was looking behind them.

"Just get us out of here!" pleaded Jern. Wil jerked the controls and the fighter spun out of the bay into space.

"Good job!" exclaimed Jern. "We're leaving them in the vapor!"

Wil tried to pull the ship out of its spin but instead put it into a tumble. As they tumbled and spun through space, the men yelled, half from the wild ride and half from joy as they put increasing distance between themselves and the Dominion destroyer.

When Lam regained consciousness, it was night, and he could not see any of his surroundings. He groaned and winced as he tried to move and found that he was still tied and lying face down in the dirt. He could tell that he was bruised and bleeding all over, and his head pounded so hard he was afraid it would split. He thought he had had it rough with the Doomen?

"Max?" he croaked.

"I'm here, Lam," he whispered back hoarsely. "But I wish I weren't. The natives didn't waste any time in greeting us."

Lam moaned, then asked, "What sort of creatures are they?"

"They look like wild animals. They barely walk on two legs, and they're covered with long gray fur." Maxai paused to catch his breath, then continued, "They have long snouts and carnivorous teeth. They seem primitive, but are skilled enough to disarm and capture us."

Lam lifted his head as much as the pain would allow and squinted through the darkness. The woods were not as thick here; the spot seemed to be a clearing. Scattered around were mounds of stone and earth with dark spots Lam thought might be openings. Surrounding the entire clearing was a wall of piled stone.

"Now we know what happened to the last people who landed here," whispered Lam. Then after a moment he added, "Do you think they've left us alone?" He guessed that Maxai had been conscious longer and might know more of what was happening.

"I think so."

"See if you can roll toward me and I'll try to loosen your ropes," Lam whispered. Lam heard Maxai squirm until he was back to back with Lam. Lam strained at the knot binding Maxai's hands. "It's gotten tight from pulling you," he explained. After a few moments of groping with his almost-numb fingers, he figured out the knot and began to tug on the loop.

"They're coming back!" whispered Maxai urgently. Lam squinted in the direction of the mounds and thought he saw movement. He pulled harder, but the knot refused to give. Sweat began to build on his brow as he worked at what he saw as their only hope for escape.

"I think it might be getting looser," whispered Lam to Maxai after a few more moments of work.

"I pray the Source that it is," answered Max.

Although his ears pounded with the exertion and pain, Lam could hear the muffled footsteps of his approaching captors.

When Lam craned his neck to look up, he saw that he and Maxai were surrounded by the creatures that had captured them. He continued to struggle against the knot, more from desperation than any conviction that it would do any good.

One of the creatures, Lam could tell through the dark, seemed to be wearing something around its neck. The creature pointed at Lam and made a growling, grunting noise; another approached Lam and kicked him in the face. Lam screamed from the pain, and from anger and frustration. The furry creatures seemed to scream too.

The one with something around its neck bent over and cautiously approached Lam, staring into his face. As it drew near, Lam could see that the object suspended from its neck was one of their pistols. It reached out one of its thick, padded fingers and touched Lam's face. Lam realized that he must look and sound very strange to the furry beings. Seeing a flat, furless face was quite a novelty.

The one with the pistol hanging from its neck again made some grunts and noises, and the other creatures proceeded to poke at Lam's face. It seemed to be funny—the creatures began making strange noises that Lam guessed were laughs.

"I don't find it so funny," muttered Lam.

"My hands are free," announced Maxai.

After the news had sunk in, Lam delivered their strategy. "If we can lure the one with the pistol toward you, maybe you could grab the pistol and shoot us out of this predicament."

"I don't know," Maxai responded. "But we've got to do something."

The creature with the pistol was apparently not happy with the chatter, and he sent one of the others to deliver a blow to Maxai. However, before it came within kicking range, Maxai began singing, making strange noises with his lips, and performing whatever tricks he could think of that would make the pistol-wearer curious enough to approach. It kept staring at Maxai, but it was not coming. Maxai started to make quieter sounds.

The creature turned its head to one side and then started shuffling nearer. It stopped slightly more than an arm's length from Maxai, but would come no closer.

"Source, help me! It'll have to be now," whispered Maxai. He leaped to his feet and grabbed the blaster. The creature howled and jerked back. Maxai struggled to pull the precious weapon off the creature's neck.

"Look out!" shouted Lam. The warning did not help; Maxai was immediately knocked to the ground by other creatures and tied again.

The leader, the one with the pistol, made angry-sounding noises. The other creatures responded by dragging the prisoners around the outside of the clearing. This time the pain was even worse; the men were being pulled over old bruises and scratches.

Moments later they reached a group of stone structures, the ones they had seen from a distance. These were mounds of stone and earth with one small opening in each. Each mound was backed up against the stone wall so that together they formed a half circle. In the center of the mounds was a large pile of stones flattened at the top with several steps leading to the plateau. The prisoners were hauled roughly up the steps and dropped near the center. Several of the creatures circled them. Lam could see that more creatures were emerging from the mounds and were circling on the ground below them. Their howls blended with the other night sounds of animals and insects to provide a frightening backdrop to the ritual which centered on them.

"Max, this is an altar," muttered Lam in despair as he realized the significance of the stone pile he lay on.

"Source, forgive me!" cried Maxai in a similar despair. "I should have trusted instead of making the foolish attempt at the pistol."

The leader of the creatures had just mounted the steps and was approaching them. In its hands it carried a large stone knife.

Lam felt the stone beneath him and noticed a slimy coating. *Blood*, he thought to himself.

"We're going to be sacrificed!" screamed Lam. "Source, be with us!" he called with resignation in his voice.

The creature approached Maxai first and held the knife high. He howled the most blood-curdling scream Lam had ever heard. The others responded. The stone blade glinted in the moonlight as the creatures continued their ritual.

Lam closed his eyes. He could not watch. He tried to picture himself in Starjumper, comforted by the hum of her engines, watching the dazzle of stars through his viewing port. He tried to feel his ship, but all he felt was cold stone and all he could hear were the strange noises of the creatures preparing to spill blood for their deity.

Then Lam thought he could hear something else. Perhaps it was just the ringing in his ears. The creatures stopped howling. Lam feared that they had finished their ritual and were ready to begin the sacrifice, but they seemed to have lost interest in their prisoners. They were looking into the forest, their heads tilted. Lam looked at the creatures closest to him and could see their pointed black noses were searching the air.

Suddenly the clearing was flooded with a brilliant blue light and an intense harmonic sound that vibrated in the trees. The creatures screamed and covered their eyes. Most of them leaped from the stone altar and dove into the mounds.

The leader, with one arm covering his eyes, reached for the pistol that hung around his neck. Lam and Maxai looked into the clearing and saw that the light came in rays that moved like the spines of a living creature. The light and un-human music drew closer. The gray-furred leader took the pistol off its neck and held it toward the light. It pulled the activator but instead of shooting at the light, accidentally hit one of its fellows. With their leader now also a threat, the few remaining creatures leaped from the table and ran to the mounds. The creature with the pistol tried again, but did not understand how to aim it. It shot its own foot and howled all the way to the mounds.

The light came nearer. It bathed them all. Lam felt an amazing sense of warmth and comfort. As his eyes adjusted he could see that the light came from a pile of stones on a crude wooden wagon. Surrounding the cart, and singing as they pulled, were apparently more inhabitants of the planet, but Lam could tell even from a distance that they did not look like the crude creatures that had captured them.

The wagon stopped at the base of the altar and the rescuers ascended the stairs. As they walked toward him, Lam felt like joining in the harmony; Maxai already was—as well as his hoarse throat would let him. Lam was overcome by it all—the light, the music, and these creatures approaching them. They were tall, strong-looking beings covered with short brown fur. Their heads were large and shaped like a deer's. They had large, dark eyes that shone in the blue light. On powerful legs they walked toward the men. One gathered up Maxai in its slender arms. Another approached Lam. As Lam was being carried down the steps, he felt a deep sense of peace as the gentle creature held him close to its warm body. As they returned to the source of the light, Lam realized his extreme fatigue. He hummed along with the harmony a little bit, and then fell asleep.

Maxai felt the same drowsiness. The M-stone in his amulet glowed fiercely, shining even in the bright blue light from the stones on the wagon. The rescuers laid their charges on the cart carrying the stones that emitted the light. The light was so intense it shone through their bodies. One of the kind creatures walked up to the cart and surveyed their sleeping charges. It tipped its head to one side, and then the other, gazing at them with large dark eyes that sparkled in the blue brilliance. After a few moments, it raised its arm and lowered it. The cart creaked and began to move as the creatures started their return trip.

Chapter Seventeen

Hang on! I'm going to try this one," declared Wil.

"Why not? It's the only one you haven't tried," replied Jern.

Wil responded to his quip by handing him the Emec card from their old fighter. "Here, plug this in," instructed Wil as he began pressing colored bars on the ship's control panel. Moments before, they had managed to untie each other's hands. Now they both held their breath as Wil pressed the last bar in the sequence.

"That's it!" shouted Jern as a three-dimensional star system map with eliptical grids appeared on the screen before them.

Wil sighed after his initial excitement had subsided.

"I sure wish I understood this bird better," he said turning to Jern. "Are we being followed yet?"

"No. I guess they gave up when they saw our skills in take-off. Actually, I think we're getting the hang of this thing."

"I suppose they figure we're going to crash into an asteroid anyway, so they won't have to worry about us," joked Wil. Then after a few moments he added, "It looks as if we're all set. If we can just get this thing between the satellites, we'll be on our way to Refuge."

Wil and Jern had been careening toward the light gate since their escape from the destroyer. They were still only barely in control, but it appeared they were getting close to a final escape.

"Get ready," warned Wil. "If this works, we'll be de-massed momentarily."

"Oh! Oh! I guess they didn't give up on us!" cried Jern, scanning the rear viewing port.

"The Power guide us," declared Wil. "There's no way they

can catch us now." Their ship nearly hit the corner satellite in the light gate, but managed to pass through and began to shimmer. Doomen fighters, launched from the damaged destroyer, began firing upon the stolen vessel. The red bolts were right on the mark but passed straight through the ghostly fighter—it had de-massed. The image of the ship thinned out and became brighter. With a flash it was gone.

Kurdon sat with clenched fists in his silent, private quarters on the destroyer. Sporadically he received progress reports on the repairs. Metal workers, technicians and electrical personnel had been working for hours to repair the extensive damage from the two fiery explosions. These were the major repairs just to make the destroyer operational again; minor repairs would continue for weeks. For a long time he stared, focusing on nothing in the room. His intense meditation was broken by a technician who ran into the room after knocking for admittance. He was one of Kurdon's personal crew that worked on his flagship.

"Exalted Kurdon," he related, catching his breath. "We have completed our initial analysis of the Tsuian navigational code. We believe we have assembled the proper program to follow the enemy to their destination gate."

Kurdon, who had not looked at the technician, now turned to face him.

"Are you sure?" Kurdon demanded softly.

The technician opened his mouth as if to qualify his remarks, but then said simply, "Yes."

"Good." Kurdon turned to one of his human body guards who wore a light-colored padded armor and ordered, "Have Scurvit summon the commanders of all ships to be battle-ready and prepared to de-mass on the next orbit."

Chapter Eighteen

Before Lam even opened his eyes, he could tell daylight had come. Light warmed his battered body and birds sang all around him. The sun was so bright, now filtering through his closed eyes, that he moved his hand to shield them before he opened them.

"So, you finally decided to wake up," chided Maxai when he saw that Lam was beginning to shift around. "It looked as though I would have to load you on a raft and float you back to the camp." Lam shook his head, not quite comprehending what Maxai was talking about.

"Actually," admitted Maxai, who was sitting near Lam on the forest floor, "I just woke up myself." Lam squinted blankly, still groggy. He knew he was alive and that every piece of his body hurt—that's all. Then he looked around. They were on the beach near a stream. Tall trees towered above, ferns grew around them, and a small fire crackled nearby. In the wall of the forest a short distance away, a trail opened.

"Where are the . . . the . . ." stammered Lam, not knowing the words for their rescuers.

Maxai put his hand on Lam's shoulder and tipped his head toward the woods. Lam's eyes still had not fully focused, but as he gazed in the direction Maxai indicated, he could see a pair of brown eyes staring at him. The creature's body blended in perfectly with the background. Looking around, he could see several other pairs of eyes.

"There are quite a few out there. What are they doing?" asked Lam.

"Maybe they're shy," suggested Maxai.

"I suppose, but they certainly weren't shy last night," observed Lam, remembering the awful reality of last night's nightmare.

"We are grateful for what you did last night," Maxai called out gently. "We would like to thank you in person." There were some faint rustlings from the woods, and it seemed that some of the eyes moved closer.

"We came a long distance to be here, and we are happy we are with you," he continued. Again there was a faint rustling. Moments later a small, brown fur-covered creature with large brown eyes was touching Maxai's ripped clothing with its long, delicate fingers. Neither Maxai nor Lam had seen or heard it coming; it seemed to appear from nowhere. Soon there were others around them, standing and staring at them with their large brown eyes. Some were bold enough to approach the strangers and sniff them or touch them.

Lam inspected them closely. They had powerful legs and cloven hoofs instead of feet. Apart from their legs, they were very slender. Their heads were slightly oversized, it seemed to Lam, and their faces had a sort of muzzle.

Soon the adults began to emerge from the cover of the forest. One of the first continued walking toward the men. He stopped when he reached Lam and Maxai.

"Thank you for rescuing us," declared Lam, as gently as he could. The creature tipped its head to one side a little. Then it spoke. Its voice was at once like the singing of birds and the sighing of the wind through the trees. Lam found it indescribably beautiful, but could not understand a word of it, if indeed there were words. Then the creature pointed to itself and spoke only two syllables. It then pointed to the others around them and repeated the sounds. Lam knew it was telling him the name of their tribe, or race.

Lam tried to repeat it. "Le-in," he enunciated. The creature's eyes danced, and the smaller ones erupted with sounds like bubbling water. Lam turned and laughed with Maxai.

"I could get a job entertaining the creatures on this planet," he laughed again. Soon they were all laughing. Laughter was one thing they all understood. Then one of the Le-in children

132

walked to Lam and held out Padu's amulet that Lam had been carrying in his pocket.

"It must have fallen out of my pocket," Lam remarked as he accepted the amulet.

The white stone was glowing more brilliantly than it ever had before. The child looked up toward the Le-in that had spoken with Lam, pointed to the amulet and spoke in his forest-tongue. The adult nodded his head and took from a pouch strapped around his waist another amulet, a simple Monobarite stone tied to a leather strap. The creature placed it around his neck and came closer to Lam. He held out his arms and extended his delicate hands, palms up. Lam looked at the Le-in and reached out his hands. Lam carefully touched his fingers to the Le-in's. There was a crack and a flash like an electric shock. Maxai and Lam gasped in surprise.

"Well, this is the place—" announced Wil. "I hope." They had just re-massed at the Refuge gate.

"I don't see them," observed Jern. "But I suppose I wasn't really expecting to. Where do we go now?"

"We're obviously in a solar system," noted Wil, pointing to the sun shining brightly on the viewing screen. "Refuge must be orbiting around here somewhere."

"Do you think you can work the scanner on this thing to pick up any energy output from the fleet?" asked Jern.

"Are you kidding? It's only by the Power I can even steer it!"

The two sat in thought for a moment, Wil gazing at the viewing screen and Jern out the port. Jern broke the silence.

"Do you see that bluish-white spot? It's larger than the rest—it must be a planet."

"Yes, I see it."

"That color sometimes means there is water on it."

"So you think that's it?"

"Like you said, it has to be around here somewhere."

"Let's go—or try to anyway," said Wil, still not confident about his Doomen fighter piloting.

"I hope we find them soon," mentioned Jern. "We haven't eaten in years."

"It sure seems like it," admitted Wil.

"It seems bluer the closer we get," observed Wil as the ship continued to hurtle toward the sphere they hoped was Refuge.

"Uh, I think you're right."

"That's got to be it. I would say it must have water. Whether the fleet is there or not, I'd like to jump in a nice cool pond right now," Wil conveyed longingly.

Soon they were orbiting the planet. They had agreed to circle the planet once to see if the fleet might be there.

"Look there—on the horizon!" exclaimed Jern from his post by the viewing port.

"What?" asked Wil, but even as he spoke he saw it too—flashes of light. It was the sun reflecting off the hulls of the fleet. Cheering and praising the Source, the two were nearly in tears as they sped toward the fleet.

"This is Patrol One calling base," summoned a Tsuian into his fighter's com-link.

"Go ahead, Patrol One."

"There's a vessel approaching the fleet—I think it's a Doomen fighter!"

Moments later the entire fleet of Tsuian fighters was in space, ready for a battle. "This is Defense Leader, take the attack plan 'hyperbol' and wait for my signal to fire."

The fighters spread out, forming a ring that would encircle the Doomen ship. Moments later they were within range.

"Try the com-link!" yelled Jern. They had only just realized their Doomen ship would not be welcome.

"This is Wil and Jern, your friends. By the Source, do not fire!" There was no answer.

"No good!" cried Wil to Jern. "They probably don't even have the same transmission technology, let alone the same frequency."

"Fire!" ordered the Defense Leader.

The plan was for each ship to maneuver above the Doomen ship and fire once, then return to formation to let the next one fire until the target was destroyed. The first ship swept into position and fired.

"We've been hit!" shouted Wil.

"I don't think it hurt us. They're in the hyperbol formation—you can dodge the next one."

Wil flew an evasive pattern, hoping that somehow they would be able to communicate who they were before being destroyed.

"Defense Leader, this is Patrol One. Do you see the crazy way that thing is flying?"

"Yes. It looks as if they're out of control. I couldn't have done that much damage when I hit it. I don't get it; Doomen are better pilots than that."

"This is Defense Leader to all patrols. Hold your fire, but be on alert."

"They've stopped firing!" yelled Jern. "Do you remember your light code?"

"Yes!" shouted Wil. "Do you? Hit the cabin lights."

Jern sprang to the light control and began to flash the lights on and off. The patrol, if they noticed, would recognize it as the Tsuian code call for help.

"This is Defense Leader. Does anyone else see that ship's lights blinking?"

"Yes. It looks like the emergency light code."

"This is Defense Leader. Let's flank the ship and bring it back to the fleet and find out what's going on."

Chapter Nineteen

Our last report from Hud and Melena was that Lam and Maxai went to check a clearing for more ships," stated Haml. "They were supposed to return right away—but they haven't shown up yet."

"I hope nothing has happened to them," Wil remarked. Just being back among their comrades was an unimaginable delight and miracle, especially as they recounted the stories of their adventures, which then passed from ship to ship in the fleet orbiting the planet. That the Source had worked was a marvelous understatement. But Wil had hoped he would see everyone when he rejoined the fleet. He was disappointed to learn that his sister was on the planet and that Lam and Maxai were missing.

"Do you know where they landed?" asked Jern.

"Oh, yes," assured the burly Haml, who had been appointed leader of the orbiting fleet. He stood beside Wil and Jern as they ate in his quarters on the carrier. "We have that location. As a matter of fact, two fighter crews are down there searching for them. They splashed down right after Starjumper landed, but we haven't heard from them since you arrived."

Wil looked at Jern and could tell they were thinking the same thing.

"Care to join me?" asked Wil.

"Of course," Jern responded.

"Could we trade in a slightly used Doomen fighter for a ship with instructions in plain Tsuian?" humored Wil.

"Of course," Haml said, mimicking Jern.

Their ship landed with a splash in the lake as the other fighters had done and Wil and Jern navigated it to the shore.

They jumped into the knee-high water and pulled their craft as far ashore as they could.

"At times like this I wish we had put gravity resistors in these things," panted Jern as they heaved. Once the ship was secure, they drew their pistols and walked to the clearing where the other ships were resting. Finding each ship vacant, they paused in the clearing to decide what to do next.

"I don't see a sign of anyone," declared Jern.

"Neither do I. There are no roads or trails. Maybe they decided to walk down this beach."

"But why would they be so late in reporting in?"

Wil surveyed the surroundings, hoping to find a clue. Then he thought he heard it—a sound coming from the forest.

"Do you hear that?" asked Wil pointing toward the forest.

Jern nodded. Suddenly the commotion grew louder and they saw something move. Jumping behind a fallen log, they aimed their pistols at the forest edge and waited breathlessly.

"Melena!" shouted Wil, dropping his pistol. The noise had been caused by the landing party returning to the site. Wil and Jern vaulted over the log and ran to meet the group. The members of the landing party had been laughing and talking, but now stood electrified and motionless as they watched the two men they presumed dead, or at least captured, run toward them. Melena tearfully embraced Wil, then Jern, and then Wil a second time.

"I couldn't feel you on the Other Side!" she cried. "But I have not been able to feel the Other Side much these last years. Thank the Source I have you with me yet a while longer."

"I was ready for the Other Side, believe me," choked Wil shakily. "Have I got a story to tell you."

But the story was interrupted as Lam and Maxai stumbled out of the woods behind them. Wil and Jern ran to greet them, while Lam and Maxai limped along as fast as they could to return the greeting.

"We thought you were dead!" exclaimed Lam.

"We thought you were lost," quipped Jern. "You two look awful!"

Melena and the others joined the celebration of the recently rescued.

"They have a story to tell you, too," winked Melena to Wil and Jern.

Lam spent the evening directing the landing of shuttles and small craft. The space sick came first, and then those who would be able to gather food and water to stock the ships. That night the Tsuians held the thanksgiving service that had been delayed by the capture of the first landing party the evening before. Lam was able to convince a few of the Le-in to join them. It took a great deal of courage to leave the forest and be in the open with such strange creatures as Lam and the Tsuians must have seemed to them. Laii, the apparent leader of the Le-in, who had carried Lam to safety and who carried a Monobarite amulet of his own, sat next to Lam at the service.

The service began with singing as the wide-eyed Le-in looked on. Everyone sat on logs arranged in a half-circle around a large fire that illuminated the faces of the worshipers and reflected off the metal surfaces of the closest ships. The vigorous songs were followed by quieter songs that at times seemed to be accompanied by the crackling of the fire and the nighttime sounds of the forest. Lam felt more comfortable joining in with the Tsuians' worship: probably because he felt a kinship with them after all they had been through together.

This was the closest Lam had gotten to actually listening and watching a group in worship. Relaxing by the fire, he found it disarming. Hud and a few younger Tsuians played on stringed instruments that used a twelve-note scale, and the singers vocalized in a complicated harmony that sounded both joyful and mysterious.

Lam attemped to interpret for the Le-in, using gestures and the few simple words he had learned from the forest people. As he strove to interpret the deep and personal meanings of the words, he became aware of a desire within himself to feel the joy these people felt. But he still did not understand how to receive it.

To Lam's astonishment, the Le-in seemed to understand it all perfectly. Their excitement rose until they burst into their own song. The music was so different, and so beautiful, that the Tsuians stopped singing.

Hud whispered to the musicians, "They seem to worship the Source and the Power too. Their voices seem to be led by the Power. What can we do?" The musicians began accompanying the Le-in. The effect was very extraordinary and very beautiful. Neither the Le-in nor the Tsuians had ever experienced music quite like it.

During the days that followed, the natives and newcomers quickly became friends, and Lam continued to learn the language. Lam's experience in many dialects helped him quickly acquire a basic understanding of the language.

Constantly surrounded by two groups of people who believed in the Source, Lam became sullen as he reflected on his life. He was hounded by the thought of whether to believe in the Source as they did. To add to his trouble, he had been spending time with Melena on walks, or working with her, and had become aware of her beauty. Late one afternoon, as Hud and Lam were laying their armloads of edible roots on their cart at the edge of the woods, Lam decided to talk to Hud about it.

"I don't know what we would have done without the Le-in," remarked Hud. "There is enough wild food on this planet to last quite a while and still leave plenty for our forest friends."

"My neck appreciates them more," Lam joked. Then he paused and took a deep breath. "In fact, there are many things I like about this planet and the people on it. You know, I appreciated your brother, even when he frustrated me. We could talk. And, I feel I can talk to you, too."

"Good," reflected Hud with a smile. He leaned on the wagon and gave Lam his attention.

"Melena and I have been spending quite a bit of time together . . ." Lam started a bit shakily.

"She's a wonderful woman," assured Hud.

"She makes me want to be with her more and more. Do you know what I mean?" Lam hoped Hud would understand, because he was having trouble explaining it.

Hud smiled gently when he realized what Lam was trying to express.

"I think it is very important that you talk to Melena about this," Hud counselled.

"I was afraid you'd say that," groaned Lam, shaking his head. "It's hard enough to talk to you."

"I still think you'd better," Hud again warned gently.

That evening, Lam stood next to Melena around one of the cooking fires, along with Wil and several others. They were sipping a warm drink made of steeped leaves and lake water; the air cooled quickly as the sun set.

"Care to join me for a little walk up Gray Hill?" asked Lam. It was a path they had taken several times to relax and watch the activity of the camp below. They called it "Gray Hill" because of its large slate areas over which a river fell, cascading its silver water down the side of the hill to a pool below. From the top the view of the lake and countryside was spectacular.

Melena smiled and they struck off down the path toward the hill.

"Things are going well," Melena encouraged. "Soon we'll be able to handle another space voyage, or we can bring our people here to dwell until it's safe to return to Tsu."

Lam nodded in agreement, but his mind was doing spins trying to decide what to say to her.

"I've noticed you've become rather solemn lately," said Melena, changing the subject for Lam. He shrugged.

After a few moments he said, "I suppose I have." They had reached the hill and were starting to walk up a trail near the lower falls.

"Do you want to talk about it?" asked Melena.

Lam laughed and commented, "Yes and no." He took a deep breath and began, "It seems like years ago, but it has not been so long since I first met your father on Saan. I've been through a lot since then, and I've seen some pretty incredible things, too many coincidences—such as the last one: being rescued by the Le-in who just happen to also worship the Source. Not only that, I've seen how, well, content you all are—you and the Le-in. You know? It seems that things can be going badly and you're still *content*. I'm not sure I have ever felt that way, certainly not since I was a child. I'm left wondering what in the galaxy is going on as I see races that live on opposite sides of the galaxy get together and sing to the same deity."

Lam laughed again and added, "I'm just a bit confused, you might say."

Melena smiled warmly. "You've begun to notice that things happen when we pray," she noted. "It may sound funny, but I've been praying that you would."

Lam and Melena laughed together as they reached the top. Standing on an outcropping of slate that overlooked the valley to the left and the camp to the right, they could already see the early evening stars. They sat down on the ledge and drank in the forest air, letting the wind caress their faces and toss their hair.

Finally Lam felt ready, took a deep breath and confessed, "I told your father about my past, but I've been keeping it from you."

"You're Entarian," Melena replied. She took his hand, knowing that the name of his planet renewed in him the old pain.

"How come everyone seems to know already?" asked Lam, somewhat angry, but relieved he did not have to tell that part of his story over again.

"Your accent, the way you hid things, your hate for the Dominion—" Lam put his hand over her mouth and chuckled.

"Okay, so I'm transparent. I'm also a criminal—or was. I raided Dominion vessels as a member of the pirate cartel."

Melena did not appear shocked. "I assumed it was something like that," she reassured. "But your life is changing." Lam smiled in agreement and they turned their attention to the camp below, now dark except for the flickering cooking fires. Once more he took a deep breath to relax and determined to broach the final touchy subject of the evening.

"That's not the only thing troubling me." Melena gazed at Lam as he spoke, but he stared out over the valley. "Ever since that day on Tsu when I first saw you, I thought you were very beautiful. And as we've traveled together I've grown quite fond of you." Wishing he'd never started in, Lam added awkwardly, "I don't know how, or even if I should, say anything more. I—I—"

Melena put her hand on his shoulder. "I think I know what you are trying to say. I am fond of you, too." Lam wondered what *she* meant by "fond"; in any case, the tone of her voice told him there was a "but" coming anyway. Melena continued, "And that is *true*. But Lam, how old do you think I am?"

Lam pondered for a moment and replied, "About 25 or 30."

"Our years are a little shorter than yours, but not much. I am years older than you."

Lam shook his head and laughed nervously. "Are you kidding?"

"No, Lam, I'm serious. You and I are very different. Our races are similar physically, and of course we have been through many of the same emotions lately. But when each of our races was created by the Source, what happened in their relationship with Him determined how they could live. We have always walked in the Power with the Source, and things are very different for us. We live to be very old, and unless someone takes our life by violence, we give our lives up when we are called and enter life in what we call the 'Other Side.' That is why we do not fear our own deaths—or did not until the Doomen conquered Tsu. I do not know your race's history. But I know that in this way we are very different."

Lam was beginning to feel crushed. Not only did he feel separated from Melena, but his own life apart from the Source was being magnified by her words.

"But what about the changes and fears you mentioned?" questioned Lam.

"Yes," she admitted with sadness in her voice. "It began when the Dominion began to rule Tsu. Some of our people fell to the lure of personal power and gain that the Dominion offered. Oh, they disguised it as a way to help our people, but really it was disobedience to the Source. The very presence of the Doomen seemed to release fear and death."

"I believe you," said Lam softly, "but I don't understand what difference it makes. How old did you say you were?"

Melena smiled and said, "Very old—but young for a Tsuian."

The two sat silently for a long while. Melena did not know what to do for Lam. He was an eternity away from her, and she did not know how to bring him the peace or answers he obviously yearned for. She prayed silently.

Hearing soft footsteps behind them, they turned and discovered Laii had joined them. He waved his hand over the scene below them and above them and made some whispering sounds.

"Yes, it is very beautiful," answered Lam.

Laii looked at Lam, and Lam in turn met Laii's gaze. The large, dark eyes looked very serious, and he put a hand on Lam's head. He made a soft chirping sound and Lam replied, "Yes, I am your friend."

Laii then made more motions and sounds and Lam looked puzzled. Melena said, "Do you understand him?"

"I understand the words, but I don't understand the meaning. He is referring to the Source and the Power. He uses different terms, but I know that is what he means—but in the same breath he is saying 'friend.' I don't know if he means my friends worship the Source, or that I'm his friend and I should, or what."

Laii could tell he was still not being understood, so he launched into a story using gestures and simple words. Lam translated for Melena as Laii spoke.

"Before—I don't know how long ago he means—but before today anyway, the Le-in worshiped the Source and the Power. Then something bad happened. I can't understand what, but the Source was apparently very angry with them, but he still was not angry with them, if that is possible."

Melena interrupted, "Oh, yes. He can still love someone but be angry with their behavior."

"But this trouble lasted a long time. Then the Friend came. I don't know what friend. The Friend came and made them happy." Lam gave a puzzled look at Melena and then said to Laii, "Thank you for that. I don't really understand, but maybe I will. It sounds important, and it obviously is to you."

After a while, Melena and Laii decided to leave, but Lam chose to stay a while so he could think. There were so many pieces that didn't seem to fit together. He sat alone on the stone, a warmer-than-usual breeze caressing his face. As he laid his head against some moss, the word "friend" kept running through his mind. Not meaning to, he fell asleep.

He dreamed he was back on Saan, but during the day in the desert. The wind was hot against him, and occasionally a gust of wind would blow stinging sand against his face. His eyes were sore from the bright sun and he was very thirsty. Even worse, he was gripped by an indescribable combination of emotions: fear, loneliness, guilt—all transformed into an almost physical force that constricted his chest and reached down into his throat and squeezed. In desperation he called out the only word that came to his mind: "Friend! Friend!"

The wind grew stronger, forcing him to the ground. Swirling sand stung his skin and eyes; he had trouble breathing. Trembling with panic, he felt something suddenly grab his shoulders and begin to drag him across the sand. Lam wanted to scream but could not. Soon the surroundings became dark and quiet. A cool breeze refreshed his skin. Opening his eyes, he saw that he had been brought into a cave. A man was seated beside him on a stone and was pouring water from a flask into a cup. He handed it to Lam.

After he had drunk, Lam said, "Thank you." The man smiled and nodded. They observed each other. Lam seemed to recognize him from somewhere. "Who are you?" he asked.

The man answered with a calm, warm voice that seemed to reach into Lam's soul and bring it peace.

"I am your Friend."

"I think I recognize you, but I still can't think exactly why."

The man who claimed to be Lam's friend sat silently for a moment, studying Lam, or perhaps allowing Lam to study him. He was an older man, but strong; his appearance was something like Padu's. He had a kind face but sand clung to his eyebrows and hair. His clothes were worn and dirty as if he had traveled a long way in the desert.

"I have always been near you," said the man.

"I knew your parents; and I knew you when you were just a feeling in their hearts. I cried with you when they died—when the Dominion destroyed your planet. I traveled the galaxy with you and came with you here."

Lam could not recall an awareness of anyone being with him all these years, but the feeling of recognition remained. And this unknown "friend" seemed to know everything about him. He must know the anger Lam had toward the Dominion and the emptiness he had known during the long years after Entar was destroyed. He must know that Lam had been a pirate and even that Lam had killed in his zeal to raid Dominion vessels.

As the two pairs of eyes searched each other, Lam knew that it was true. He broke down and wept. For the first time in his life, he blurted out his failings and fears. He begged the man to help him lest the crushing weight of wasted years take his life even now.

"I am a man like you," pronounced the Friend. "I have felt everything you have and more. There is no excuse for the life you have led, and you know that too well. But there is a remedy for it: Believe that I am your Friend."

"But—but—who are you?" Lam called through his sobs.

"I am the Source. I am the Power. I am your Friend."

When Lam awoke, he felt as if he had slept an eternity. His eyes were swollen and damp—he *had* cried. Stiffly he sat up. The sun was just now lancing the sky with color and his hilltop retreat was the first to receive its warmth. He wondered to himself what had happened.

He remembered his heart-rending and almost unbelievable conversation with Melena; his strange conversation with Laii; and his dream. . . . Yes, his dream about the Friend. Everything was starting to make sense. Although he had heard more, he felt he understood something of what it meant. His haunting dreams, the strange feelings, the longings, they had all been for the Friend. The Friend. For the first time in his life he felt he was not alone.

Lam was both excited and afraid when he returned to camp. He was excited that the Friend knew everything about him and still accepted him; and he was excited by his new feeling of freedom. But he was afraid it would not last.

The others noticed a change in him almost immediately. Lam did not say anything at first when he was greeted by Wil and Hud who were lingering over a warm breakfast drink at a fire ring near the trail to the hills.

After some routine greetings, Wil asked point blank: "Lam, what did you find on the hill?"

Chapter Twenty

We have to know more," insisted Hud, shaking his head. Melena was bent over next to Hud on the lakeshore as they cleaned the large kettles in which they had been boiling fruit. She had told him about her talk with Lam the night before, and what Laii had told them about the Friend.

"But doesn't it make sense, Uncle?" argued Melena. "We can feel the Source—we always have. But what about people like Lam? There has to be a way for the Source to break through to them. You've seen what's happened in Lam's life."

Hud scooped up a handful of sand and dropped it into the pot and began to scrub the sticky remains. "The Council meets again later, and I promise we will discuss it. It is an incredible thing if it is true. Never to our knowledge has there been a physical meeting of flesh and the Source."

Melena paused to let her kettle fill with the water warmed by the afternoon sun.

"I hope it proves to mean something," Melena said quietly. "I don't know how the others feel, but ever since the Dominion came, I have felt, well, as though the Source were a little farther from me. I can no longer sense as clearly those on the Other Side. I don't know how all this about the Friend can help, but maybe it can. I hope so, anyway."

As Hud and Melena laid their kettles on the sand to dry, Hud considered the awesome matter awaiting discussion. Had the Source come physically to these gentle forest people? Had the fleet been guided here so they could learn about it?

"It doesn't feel hot," said Lam to Laii in the Le-in's language. They were standing near the woods with the cart the Le-in had used to rescue Lam and Maxai from the Krakaa. It was piled with M-stones, some quite large, and each more clear and more brilliant than any the Tsuians had.

"It is not fire," Laii replied in his song-like language. "But it can give warmth; it can bring light; and it can make you think further. It is the way the Source helps us."

Lam sent a puzzled look toward Laii as he stood resting his hands against a heap of Monobarite. Lam realized that the Le-in, however primitive they may have seemed, knew more about the stone than the Tsuians. What Laii said about thinking farther confused him.

"I do not understand," declared Lam.

"When the Krakaa come, we think we do not want them to come. Then the light comes and the Krakaa do not," explained Laii carefully, trying to use only words familiar to Lam. "That is why they ran when we came to rescue you."

As Lam mulled over the matter, he realized that somehow the Le-in's minds controlled the actions of the stones. Or did they? What was this business about the Source?

Lam was not sure he was even understanding the Le-in correctly. What he heard did not make much sense, although he knew that the stones grew brighter when together. He turned over the facts in his mind. According to what the Le-in said, each M-stone phenomenon had to do with some sort of exertion, some sort of force or energy. Lam shortly gave up, for the time being, trying to untangle the puzzle.

He said to Laii, "I go to the shore to see my friends. We have work to do before night comes again." The friends prepared to leave the wagon at the edge of the clearing and go back to shore. Picking up the bundle of sticks and the vegetation that Laii said was good to eat, they began walking away when Lam said in Common, hoping Laii would understand from the context, "Wait a minute, I forgot my staff." Lam turned back and walked to the wagon where it was leaning.

Lam suddenly realized it was the first time he had forgotten the walking stick since he had received it on Tsu. He put more weight on his leg. It hurt noticeably less than before. He also noticed that his scrapes and bruises were healing quickly. Pausing in thought for a moment, he wondered if it had anything to do with the M-stones. He picked up his cane and returned to where Laii waited, and they walked to the camp.

That night, as Hud lay on his mattress of reeds, covered with a blanket of cloth-like leaves the Le-in had provided, he thought about the Council meeting held earlier that evening. The Council had come to no conclusion about the "Friend." They had decided each would have to consider it on his own for a while. Hud relaxed his thoughts as he looked up at the moon and listened to the fire crackle beside him. *I think I would like to meet this Friend*, he thought.

He closed his eyes and began to drift into sleep. The image of the moon still floated before his eyes, and the crackling of the fire seemed to be less random and more meaningful. The moon split and became two majestic planets drifting peacefully around their sun. Both planets rotated on their axes for thousands of years. Then from space's dark womb a large comet with spectacular colors emerged. But soon Hud could tell it was roaring directly at the planets. It swept the first planet with its tail, but the second one it hit full force. The first planet became darkened by the debris in the comet's tail. The second was knocked off its axis; earthquakes, volcanoes, terrible storms and floods devastated the planet. Worst of all, it stopped rotating and became a dead sphere.

Hud's heart ached for the planets. They seemed to be floating farther away, or shrinking. When they appeared to be the size of just small stones, a man approached them and gazed on them with pity in his eyes. He was a gentle, friendly looking man. Taking the second planet, the one with the most devastation, he dipped it in a nearby stream, then held it close to his body until it was dry. Then he breathed on it until it became green again. He flattened out his palm, placed the tiny world in it and spun it like a top. It whirled in his hand as if it had never been struck by the comet.

Holding the renewed planet, he turned to the first one. It showed less damage, having been only darkened by the comet.

He gently breathed on the planet until it was clean and bright again.

Hud was relaxing, enjoying the sight of the planets spinning lazily in space when he was horrified to see another comet coming. Much larger than the first, it was headed straight for them. The friend of the planets left them to spin on their own and stood in the path of the oncoming comet. It seemed immense and made a sound like an earthquake or terrible storm. Closing in, Hud could tell that it was nearly as big as the man. The man stood tall and braced himself for the collision. *How will he survive?* wondered Hud. The comet struck the man, causing a terrible explosion. Flames leaped into space; sparks and lightning flashes convulsed around him.

When the scene finally quieted, Hud could see that the planets were safe, but the man was dead. Hud sobbed uncontrollably. It seemed such an injustice, that one so kind would be dead. But as he watched, the man's body began to change. It seemed to melt and glow, then form into a ball and become a sun. Both planets began to orbit this new sun, and somehow the scene seemed perfect and Hud's grief turned to joy.

When Hud awoke, he found it impossible to clear the images from his mind. Stretching and opening his eyes to the morning twilight before the sun rose over Gray Hill, he propped himself on one elbow and looked about the camp. Preparations for breakfast were under way, and he breathed in the cool morning air which was mingled with the smells of cooking food. Still he could not snap out of the haunting mood that followed his dream.

Throwing off his leafy blanket and rising to his feet, Hud stretched and looked around again. Maxai was at the next fire over, helping a woman prepare a vegetable stew.

"Good morning!" called Maxai as Hud approached.

"Well, good morning to you! Tell me, how did you sleep?"

"I think I am beginning to like sleeping under the moon," answered Maxai. "I slept very well. And you?"

"A man has many dreams, and most mean nothing. But some do trouble the dreamer after he has awakened. I am troubled by a dream that I had last night." He related his dream to Maxai and added, "I am not sure what it means, if anything."

Maxai laughed uneasily when Hud was finished.

"I think we are being told something, because I had a very similar dream. I dreamed I stood on the shore of our lake and our children and some Le-in children played in the water. As I watched, I saw wakes in the water just beyond where the children swam, and whatever disturbed the water seemed to be getting closer. Then I saw what I took to be an immense arching back rising out of the water with scales and fins. It began swimming toward the children, and I knew that it intended to attack them.

"Suddenly a man I had never seen before came to the shore. I shouted to the children to come in. The Tsuian children turned and started for shore, but they could not outrun the beast. The Le-in children did not obey my voice and continued to laugh and splash. Then the man who was with me also called out with the same results. When it was apparent that none of the children would reach shore before the beast reached them, he shed his outer clothes and dove into the water. He grabbed the children and ran to shore, rushing back and forth several times, but there were still more that could not be saved. Seeing that, the man waded farther out into the water and splashed the water with his arms to attract the beast to himself, away from the children. This gave enough time for the children to reach shore, but the man was torn apart by the great beast."

Both stood silently when Maxai had finished telling his dream. Individually they did not know what their dreams could mean, but hearing one another's, they realized what it meant. The Source was telling them of the Friend, and they must tell the others.

"We believe the Source may have told us some very important things about the Friend," proclaimed Hud to the Council members gathered informally around a fire ring. "If our dreams are true as we interpret them, then he comes from the Source—in a way he is the Source, as indicated by the dream of the sun. In another way he is mortal and has given his life to bring his creation closer to himself."

The others agreed this may have been the meaning of the

dreams and were excited at the possibility.

"The Source of all creation became a person as we are?" questioned Maxai in wonderment. "I don't understand how it could happen," he stated, sighing and shaking his head to show he also was excited at the possibility.

"I think I'll go find Lam and see if he can talk to the Le-in about this," said Hud, rising from the log on which he had been sitting.

Lam was just waking. His eyes opened, saw the bright sun pouring through Starjumper's open portal, then closed again in rebellion.

"Wake up, Lam!" he heard an excited voice command. It was Hud. "We've got things to do!"

Lam sat with Melena, Hud and Maxai eating breakfast by the shore. They had been discussing the dreams, plans for the future, and whether Maxai's stew was better than the one Lam had cooked the day before.

"What about my M-stone theory?" Lam asked, adding yet another subject to the lively conversation.

"I mentioned your theory to some of our energy technicians, and they thought there might be something to what you say, Lam," answered Hud.

"Well, it sure seems to make sense. I've been trying to figure out Monobarite since I first saw it in Padu's amulet, then later when we had the pouch of it in Starjumper on the way to Tsu. It doesn't give off its own energy as Redlyn does, and it doesn't simply reflect light like the Rubon. From what the Le-in say, the Source provided it to amplify any energy applied to it, light, movement, even thought—especially when in need. And I think it has sped up the healing of my leg, as well as my bruises and scratches—so it may work with the body's energy as well."

"Is there any way to test your theory?" asked Melena.

"I think if we systematically join the stones with as many different kinds of energy as possible, we can tell easily."

Starting soon after breakfast, Lam, together with Wil, Jern and several other interested Tsuians, worked the rest of the day on the M-stone theory. They applied light, they placed fragments in the power unit of a pistol, and they even tried using the substance as a projectile.

"It appears you may be right about this stuff," Jern commented to Lam as they worked to open Starjumper's Redlyn compartment.

Melena called into Starjumper from the ground, "Are you sure you know what you're doing?"

"Since when has that stopped them?" replied Wil, who was standing next to his sister on the sand below Starjumper.

"But they don't know what will happen," insisted Melena with concern.

"There," announced Lam, stepping down from his ship. "We replaced some of the Redlyn rods with pieces of Monobarite." Jern followed, jumping down to the sand to join the others.

"I appreciate your concern," Lam expressed to Melena. "I know how much all of you want to return to Tsu, but you will need a way to protect yourselves from the Dominion—maybe this can help. If the stone is especially for needy situations, it would be difficult to create a more needy one than that before us. We may even have to face the Dominion in battle soon."

"Yes," Jern jumped in. "If they found out where we are, they could be here any day."

Melena turned to gaze out over the lake that reflected the cloudless blue sky. The forest and Gray Hill were also mirrored in its smooth surface.

"It's nice here, but I do miss home. And I know that the Dominion is powerful and far-reaching—it would only be a matter of time until they found us here."

Lam paused and scanned the lush countryside. In some ways he wished he could stay forever. He had made friends with the Le-in and respected their innocent wisdom. And, of course, here he had met the Friend.

"Maybe the stones will give us the protection or the edge we need," Wil suggested.

Melena nodded slowly and Lam turned and slapped Starjumper's hull affectionately. He did not like to look directly at Melena; his feelings for her had not gone away, and knowing that she was an old woman by his standards had not changed anything. He was also a little embarrassed because he had let her know how he felt.

A large number of people had left the orbiting ships to be on the planet. Some had come to help with provisioning the ships; others had come because their bodies could no longer handle weightlessness. It seemed as if all of them had gathered on the sand port that afternoon as Lam and Jern prepared to test Starjumper's M-stone fuel.

Starjumper's engines began to glow, and the crowd began to step away from the ship. Then they gasped collectively at what happened next. As the engines whined, the entire ship became shrouded with a blue light.

"Wil to Starjumper," Lam heard in his headset.

"Go ahead."

"Starjumper does not usually glow blue, does it?"

Startled by the question, Lam paused a moment. "No, she doesn't. I take that question to mean that it is now?"

"Yes, but there does not seem to be excessive heat or dangerous radiation emitting from it."

"Let's go, then," declared Lam. It was already an unusual flight, and they were still on the ground.

The gravity resistors were activated, and the engines began to lift the ship gracefully off the ground.

"We'll rise about twenty spans and then take off at a forty-five degree angle to the outer orbit before we really push the engines to see what effect the Monobarite has."

Afraid to leave the control of the uncertain craft to the computer, Lam took the controls in his hand. Sand blew as the ship lifted, slowly at first, and then faster until it was higher than the forest. The craft soon reached twenty spans and Lam gently pulled on the engine controls to lift Starjumper up and forward.

"Whoa!" they both shouted as Starjumper jerked forward, throwing them back against their seats. Lam had to catch his breath before he could slow the ship down.

"That's incredible!" shouted Lam to Jern. "I've never felt so much power while still under a planet's gravity."

"What are you two doing?" they heard Wil ask over the

com-link. Lam and Jern laughed as they showed off Starjumper's new ability.

"All ships are through the destination gate, Exalted Kurdon," conveyed his flagship's communications officer.

"Good," he observed contemptibly. "As soon as systems return to normal, tell the Doomen commander to ready scout ships. We must search the area for the Tsuians. Give orders that when they are located, they should report and return to the carrier. We shall decide how to deal with them when we know their position."

Kurdon rose from his seat and walked to the viewing screen. From the screen's magnification, he could see that they were in a system with several planets, the nearest one a blue-white color.

"You can't be far, and you can't hide for long. Then we shall see whose source is the greater."

Chapter Twenty-one

I wish Lam and Jern would return," sighed Melena, gazing at the clear blue sky above the trees.

"I do too," answered Wil, clanging shut the door to the fighter's Redlyn rod compartment. The gentle breeze from the lake began to dry his sweaty dark hair that had been matted to his forehead. "We're nearly done installing the Monobarite, and we have to finish our contingency plans."

"He's just like a child with a new toy," said Melena, shaking her head. "Ever since Starjumper had the M-stones put in, he's been pushing it to see what it can do."

Lam turned to Jern who was seated next to him at Starjumper's controls and noted, "One of the most exciting things about the M-stones is they make this blue shield. I want to test it out to see how well it protects the hull from heat on re-entry."

"Okay," answered Jern. "Just let me know which direction." Lam had let Jern try out Starjumper as they flew to the nearest planet so he could get used to how a ship responded with the M-stones.

"Let's start descending at about half-speed on this next orbit," suggested Lam. "Then we'll briefly apply more power to test how the hull holds up." The lifeless sphere below them seemed to turn as Starjumper swept around it in orbit.

"Coming up on the next orbit," reported Lam. Then his cheerful tone changed, "Wait, there's something strange on the screen. I'm picking up engine pulses."

Lam spoke sharply into his com-link, "This is Starjumper.

Please identify." He waited but there was no answer. Jern and Lam looked at each other.

"There weren't supposed to be any of our ships out here," Jern declared.

"We'd better approach for a visual." He pointed to the screen. "Here's the location."

Jern swung up out of the orbit slightly and they both scrutinized the viewing screen, straining to see the vessel they had detected on the planet's horizon.

"There," pointed Jern to a glint just above the planet's horizon.

"Yeah, I see it," replied Lam. The glint grew larger as Starjumper raced toward the strange craft.

Suddenly they both could see it clearly.

"Doomen!" Lam blurted in disgust. Jern pulled up and began pursuit as the Doomen fighter swept past.

"Good move," commended Lam as he pulled Jern out of the pilot's seat and grabbed the controls himself. He armed the cannons. The Doomen ship reversed course and headed back toward them.

"This one won't get back to the armada," proclaimed Lam, clenching his teeth. He pulled the activator and bolts of violet light exploded from Starjumper's forward guns, but the Doomen ship had just changed course.

"It's leaving the planet," Jern observed, puzzled.

"What in the galaxy?" shouted Lam; he slammed his hand on the control panel in fury at having missed. "I don't understand it. Doomen fighters never retreat."

Lam shook his head while he tried to decide what to tell his trembling hands to do. The reality of the situation began to hit him as hard as the surprise of first seeing the Doomen ship.

Starjumper swerved out of orbit and Lam applied more power for the pursuit. Lam watched his monitor as the distance between them shrank. Pulling the activator, more violet bolts erupted. They were still too far away to be accurate, but the gap was closing rapidly. Lam took a deep breath, switched on the weapons light guidance system and fired several times in rapid succession. The second bolt found its target, wrapped around the black fighter like talons around prey and the Doomen ship exploded, leaving only dust and shrapnel tumbling in space. A few pieces hit Starjumper's blue shield, turned white hot and disintegrated.

Lam and Jern sighed with momentary relief.

"The Dominion managed to follow us," Lam deliberated, fear creeping into his words.

"Do you think the fighter pilot had time to tell its commander it had found us?" asked Jern.

"Doomen don't have to tell each other anything—they just know it. Turn us around and get us back to the camp." Lam relinquished his seat to Jern as he spoke into the com-link, "Starjumper calling base."

"We've been waiting for you, Lam," Wil scolded.

Without any further greetings, Lam explained anxiously, "We've encountered and destroyed a Doomen fighter. I would guess the rest of the Dominion armada is near and knows we're in this system. We've got to run or make a stand."

There was silence for several moments; then Wil's voice, more sober now, responded, "We understand. Get back as fast as you can."

"Exalted Kurdon," began his communications officer, "the commander reports that our scouts have encountered the enemy on the third planet. A scout ship was pursued and destroyed. The other scouts have been recalled and the commander requests instructions."

Kurdon allowed a fleeting smile to cross his cheerless face for the first time in a long while. "Good," he uttered. "Tell the commander to send a squadron of fighters to the third planet to identify the Tsuians' exact location and assess their strength."

"Thank you, sir," replied the officer as he turned to communicate Kurdon's orders to the Doomen commander.

On Refuge, Melena and Wil ran to meet Lam and Jern where Starjumper landed.

"The fighters all have M-stones in place of some of the Redlyn rods," called Wil breathlessly as Lam lowered the ramp from his ship.

"Good," Lam answered as he stepped down to the sand and ran awkwardly with Wil and Jern to where the Council was gathered, already threshing their options.

"We have to leave," pleaded Melena. "We cannot endanger the lives of the Le-in by our presence, whatever we do." Lam agreed, imagining how guilty he would feel if the gentle Le-in were harmed because of them.

"I believe we have to fight them. We have the M-stones now—we stand a good chance," spoke another.

Hud had been listening quietly for some time and finally asserted, "Friends, we must seek the will of the Source on this matter."

The Tsuians, feeling embarrassed at their rashness, closed their eyes and left Lam looking around uncomfortably. He struggled to imagine what to do—he did not know how to pray. He decided to follow their example and close his eyes. The glow of engines and the flash of Redlyn bolts were all he saw.

"I need you now," he whispered as he thought back to his dream-meeting in the cave. He pictured himself standing in front of his Friend, looking into those kind eyes. "We have a terrible problem," petitioned Lam in his mind. "The Dominion is here. I saw their armada on Tsu—a destroyer and a carrier full of Doomen fighters. No one else has a fleet to compare, let alone our little fleet. We have to decide where to go and what to do."

The Friend looked back at him gently but with a strength that seemed to radiate from inside. Lam forgot that he was just imagining and felt he should confess his fear to the Friend.

"You know, I feel better than I ever have. For the first time I feel as if I have hope, and a reason to live. Tell me what you want me to do, because if you leave it up to me, I'll probably just run into the woods and live with the Le-in."

The Friend put his hand on Lam's shoulder. The strength of the man's hand gave Lam confidence.

"Lam," he seemed to say, "I have not brought you this far to abandon you and let you perish in space. If you will trust me, I have a purpose to work in and through your life. These people need your leadership desperately. I will give you the ability to lead my people into victory against impossible odds. This path will not be easy, and at times the way will be hard to see. Remember I am with you and I can never fail you—if you trust me. The Dominion will fall if you go in my Power."

Suddenly the vividness in Lam's mind began to fade and he realized that one of the elders had been speaking.

"It was the Friend . . ." began Lam quietly, but he did not know what else to say.

"Hud had noticed the visible change that had come over Lam as they prayed. He wondered aloud, "Perhaps the Source has chosen to work through you in this crisis. What do you think is best?"

Lam was at a loss for words at first, but then regained his thoughts. "I know you want to go back to Tsu, but to attempt it now would be suicidal. If we run and hide in the forest here, the Dominion will undoubtedly burn it all down. I think we should engage them with all our fighters now and fight them all the way back to their base planet if we can—we have the Emec program that will get us there."

The Council members glanced questioningly at each other. Melena sat motionless in thought. Jern unconsciously fingered his pistol. Wil spoke what they all were thinking.

"It's what we've been training for."

"We stand a good chance with the M-stones," added Jern.

"We could shuttle the rest of our people and our soldiers here to stay with the Le-in while our pilots fight the Dominion in space," offered Melena. The others spoke tentatively, as if they did not assume they could win, but then each comment bolstered their confidence.

"We don't have enough immunization for everyone else," warned Lam.

"Sickness is not a problem with us," Hud assured. Maxai winked at Lam and said, "See, I wasn't afraid of the shot."

Hud took a deep breath and concluded, "I don't see that we have any alternatives." He looked at the others but no one offered a different plan. Hud shook his head at the enormity of the task, then stood up straighter and announced in a calm but intense voice, "We had better get started."

"Are you sure you want to do this?" Lam asked.

Wil, who was strapping into a flight suit near the captured Doomen fighter, answered, "Well, I can't say I'm looking forward to it, but it only makes sense. I'm the only one who knows how to fly this crazy thing—even if I'm not very good at it."

"But what about her?" Lam questioned, nodding his head toward Melena who was helping some people off a shuttle that had arrived from the carrier. "You were just reunited after we thought you'd been killed . . ."

Wil looked toward Melena as he rested his helmet in the crook of his arm and moved the com-link aside.

"Tsuians are always ready to be called to the Other Side. My sister and I both know that. She'll know if I've gone and in some ways we will be even closer."

"Okay," Lam conceded, "but be careful. And let us know immediately when you see them coming; then get out of there— we don't want to shoot you down by mistake."

Wil donned the helmet. The gold colored visor reflected the forest. "You monitor that com-link."

Lam slapped Wil on the back as he boarded the insect-like craft. He then turned to instruct the other fighter pilots on their strategy for the coming conflict.

Wil guided the fighter up fairly well. He intended to stay well away from the Dominion armada—just close enough to identify their location. Since they had spotted Lam and Jern near the third planet, he guessed they might still be there, so he pointed the ship in the general direction and settled in for a long ride. His ship would be slower than the M-stone-equipped ships, but the Tsuians did not want to take a chance on the Dominion's discovering it if Wil were captured. Captured. Wil prayed he would not have to go through that again.

"The squadron has not located the enemy, and we do not pick up any regular energy readings from the planet," reported Kurdon's communications officer.

Kurdon was seated in his usual solemn upright position waiting for the squadron's report.

"Very well," he declared with the patience of a hunter who knows his quarry is cornered. He turned to the Doomen standing silently by his seat and asked, "Do the Doomen believe they are there?" The Doomen remained motionless and silent for a moment and then shook his head.

Kurdon then ordered coldly, "Send scouts to the fourth planet, and see that the armada follows them. They are most likely there. It appears to be the most habitable in the system." He leaned back in his seat, returned to his wordless meditation and waited.

"Lam, it's Wil!" shouted Jern urgently from the Starjumper. Lam was inspecting the rods outside, but could hear Wil calling. Pulling himself quickly into the ship, he heard the crackling sounds of the com-link.

"There are three of them," they heard Wil's voice say. "I caught them by surprise—they didn't realize I was the enemy." By this time Melena and Hud had also joined them. They heard more background noises and then Wil again spoke triumphantly, "And now there are two! But I wouldn't mind some help!"

"We'll alert the other fighter pilots," stated Hud with a reserved excitement. In a way it was a relief to him that it had started.

Lam and Jern, along with all the pilots, were already dressed and ready for flight. Melena quickly embraced Jern and Lam and followed Hud out of the ship as Lam threw himself into his seat and strapped in.

"What's your location?" asked Jern as he pulled the strap across his chest.

"Just above our carrier," returned Wil's breathless voice. "You'll know me. I'm the one who's flying crooked."

Starjumper's engines whined and the blue shroud enveloped the craft. Sand swirled around its pads as it lifted up to the tree tops. The engines glowed brighter and it was gone so quickly it seemed as though it had disappeared, leaving behind only a sonic boom.

Lam and Jern soon observed red and violet flashes in Star-jumper's viewing screen. As their ship neared, they could see two black fighters trying to catch a third which flew so erratically that their bolts missed each time.

"At least he makes a tough target, even if he can't fly," joked Jern dryly, grabbing the controls for the cannons they had installed from Padu's cache.

"Let's take the far one," directed Lam. Four violet bolts at once exploded from the ship. The duo could not tell how many hit, but the Doomen fighter exploded and Starjumper passed through the dust. By this time, two other Tsuian fighters had entered the fray and the last Doomen was hit. It burst apart and spun into space, pieces ripping off as it went.

Melena waved as the last wagon full of children was swallowed by the forest of Refuge. Turning toward the clearing, she watched her uncle lead the men in throwing branches, vines and leaves for camouflage over the shuttles and other non-military craft. Already having said goodbye to him, she now worked on strapping her helmet under her chin. One by one, fighter engines began to whine and the ships began to glow with their blue shields.

"Are you ready?" she heard a voice behind her. She turned to see Wil. He had returned the Doomen ship to join his sister in a Tsuian fighter.

"Is anyone ever ready for this?" she asked doubtfully, but added in a steady voice, "Yes, I'm ready."

Soon only bright specks remained in the blue of Refuge's sky to mark the engines, and only the echoes of sonic booms disturbed the peace of the planet. The reeds that swayed in the breeze at the lakeshore waved the fighters on their way.

In the darkness of space, Lam waited. All was quiet except for the pounding of his heart. The Tsuians had sixteen ships, counting Starjumper. The Dominion had two or three times that number. They also had the awesome firepower of the destroyer and the heavy armament of the carrier. He turned the strategy over in his mind. Though it was good, they would need more than their plan to win this fight. Picturing the Dominion armada in his mind, the reality of the crisis slapped him on the face, and the Friend seemed very unreal and very distant. He clung desparately to the promise alone.

The destroyer led the armada; the carrier followed. The smooth heavy armor of the great ships was broken by flashing lights, gun turrets and viewing ports, bays and communication relay towers. The destroyer resembled a huge sea beast, but instead of a tail, its stern bristled with seven engines. The fighters flanking it looked as though they might be bits of food for it to eat.

The armada stormed silently past the moon of Refuge. On the bridge of the destroyer, the Doomen commander stood silent and motionless, his feet apart and arms folded behind his back. The first officer, not a Doomen, studied the large main viewing screen. It showed the Tsuian carrier in stationary orbit above the planet. The ship appeared dark and lifeless.

"Do you think we could have surprised them, or could they have already fled?" the first officer asked the Doomen. The Doomen simply shook his head; he knew the Tsuians were out there somewhere.

At nearly the same instant, violet bolts erupted from the Tsuian carrier. In the volley, two Doomen fighters were damaged and the rest scattered. The hull of the destroyer was hit with several bolts, but suffered little damage to its massive armor. The Doomen commander nodded to his weapons officer and all the destroyer's guns of that side launched plasma bolts at the Tsuian carrier. The Tsuians continued their shooting, but the plasma bolts wrapped around the carrier and began to cut through the metal. Air and debris began to rip through the weakened hull. The two fighters hiding there left the carrier just before it exploded.

The Tsuian fighters had raced clear, knowing what the force of the explosion would be. They had armed most of their fission grenades and planted them on the carrier so that the explosion would work against the Dominion. The concussion, along with the flying shrapnel, crippled several Doomen fighters and damaged systems on the front of the destroyer. Before the Doomen fighters could regroup, the rest of the Tsuian fleet emerged from the dark side of the moon, firing as it came.

Like blue ghosts, the Tsuian ships dove toward the Doomen, fired and darted off as others did the same.

"This is incredible!" shouted Jern. "They can't keep up with us! Our blue shields seem to absorb the energy of their weapons when one of our ships is hit."

Lam's voice, determined and grim, replied, "We've got to stay clear of that destroyer until we've eliminated the fighters. I don't think even these shields could hold out against a plasma bolt."

"Use your eyes," Wil reminded his sister. "The helmet senses your eye and head movements and the ship responds to them." They were lessons they all had learned well, but they reminded each other in the heat of battle.

One Tsuian ship swooped out of a cluster of Doomen fighters. "Stay clear of the destroyer!" shouted Lam into the com-link. But the ship seemed to be out of control. He watched the short drama of the light guidance beams from the destroyer finding their mark and then delivering the plasma bolt. The fighter's blue shield glowed brighter and brighter as the bolt wrapped around it and tried to melt it to scrap metal. Lam did not wait to see what happened.

The Tsuians were flying and fighting very well, the M-stones making up for their lack of battle experience.

"Keep them scattered. Don't let them regroup!" ordered Lam excitedly into the com-link. The Doomen fighters seemed to be losing control. So many Doomen fighters were out of commission that armed shuttles and patrol ships were being sent from the carrier to help. The destroyer and carrier would fire when a Tsuian ship drew near, but the light guidance system was too slow and the risk of hitting their own ships too great for them to be engaged in much of the fighting.

The Doomen commander had dropped his hands to his side in surprise when the attack started. Again becoming still, he lifted his shadowed face to the ceiling of the bridge. The flashes of cannon fire lit up the bridge as if it were in a lightning storm. Alarms were sounding and orders were being barked by lower officers to repair breaches, contain fires, and direct weapons. Messengers and mechanics ran in and out of the lifts with recorders and fire extinguishers.

Soon after the Doomen commander raised his head, the Doomen fighters stopped spinning and darting randomly. They all swung and headed toward the destroyer.

"A retreat?" asked Jern hopefully.

"I'm afraid not," answered Lam, his spirits sinking. "They've gone to the cover of the destroyer to regroup."

"Stand by," Lam announced to his fleet.

They did not have to wait long to see the Dominion's next move. Lam watched in horror as the destroyer and carrier launched a swarm of tiny missiles.

"I've heard of these," noted Lam to his companion in a low tone. "They're 'smart' missiles that zero in on their prey and pursue it until either it or its target is destroyed."

"We were just evening out the odds against the fighters," lamented Jern in near-disbelief.

"Pair off," commanded Lam, recovering from his stunned state. This was a practiced routine. The Tsuians would fly in twos so one could protect the other.

"Fighter One," reported the ship.

"Fighter One, take Twelve," Lam directed.

One by one they paired off and began the next phase of their battle—staying alive.

Kalen stood in his cell and listened to the battle. There was shouting and alarms. The sound of tearing metal and explosions echoed through the metal skeleton of the destroyer. His guard just being called away to assist somewhere else in the ship, Kalen knew this was the opportunity he had been waiting for. He reached into his pocket and pulled out the tiny explosive. Backing into the corner of his cell and pulling the mattress of his cot over him, he rolled the grenade toward the cell door.

The grenade collided with the ener-bar and exploded with a roar, ripping out the walls on either side. Shrapnel and debris tore into the passageway and more alarms sounded. Kalen was nearly knocked out from the concussion, but he shook his head clear and pushed away his charred mattress. Rising to his feet, he stumbled through the rubble, coughing from the dust.

Slipping into the main passageway, Kalen ducked into a corner near a wall com-link. Several of the crew ran by, but when an officer approached, Kalen leaped in front of him, knocked him down with a right cross and grabbed his victim's pistol. Pulling the stunned man to his feet and shoving him against the wall, Kalen's eyes met the terrified officer's and he realized it was his friend.

"Kalen!" he gasped. "Are you crazy?"

"Shut up!" Kalen hissed through gritted teeth. "I didn't mean for this to be you, but it's too late. Call Kurdon and tell him there is an emergency that requires his personal attention on this ship." His friend hesitated and Kalen slammed the pistol's handle into his hostage's stomach. He gasped and doubled over. When he caught his breath, he delivered the message as Kalen demanded.

"Explain the nature of this emergency," said Kurdon in a calm but menacing voice.

"I can't. There isn't time. But you must come," the officer summoned. Kalen stood behind him with his arm around his hostage's neck and the pistol against his head.

"I do not follow the anonymous orders of my hirelings," retorted Kurdon angrily. Kalen could take no more. He pulled the officer away from the com-link and yelled into it.

"You servant of a slime-eater! You will pay for murdering my father!" Kalen's face was flushed and his eyes were wild as he blasted the wall com-link. The officer sat dazed on the floor where Kalen had thrown him, unable to understand or believe his friend.

Reaching into his pocket, Kalen pulled out a small black transmitter. He hesitated a moment and then pressed the button. The detonater he had hidden in the weapons room reacted perfectly.

Stunned chatter filled the helmets of the Tsuian fleet.

"What's happening? Who did that?" They stopped shooting for a moment as they watched the Dominion destroyer heave and belch debris from a huge wound that ripped larger with each explosion. The Dominion ships paused similarly at the surprising turn of events.

"Don't let up!" warned Lam with new energy. "Let's take advantage of this!"

Jern spoke to Lam in a deliberate fashion as he lanced space with violet bolts.

"Dodging and fighting the missiles and the fighters is wearing us down and getting us nowhere."

"You're right," concurred Lam. He addressed the fleet. "Forget the Doomen for a while. Our shields should hold for a few strikes. Concentrate on those missiles."

The fleet acknowledged his orders and the pairs stopped flying evasively so they could attack the missiles. Even in the first few moments this was successful. They eliminated many of the missiles and the Doomen seemed to have been caught off guard by the abrupt change in tactics. It wasn't long, however, before the Doomen took advantage of their easy targets. The black fighters would swoop past them, giving them the full force of their cannons. The blue shields glowed brightly where they were hit, but they held. The Tsuians destroyed more missiles as the objects were now coming right toward them and were fairly easy targets; but with the last pass of the Doomen some of the shields seemed to grow dimmer.

"Just before the Doomen reach us again, drop down out of the path of the missiles and give the Doomen a warm reception," Lam directed.

The black ships began their third approach and were surprised to find the fleet's attention focused on them. A dozen of them took violet bolts directly on their bellies and sprayed wreckage from the wounds.

The battle continued for what seemed an eternity. Dodging and shooting, getting hit. One Tsuian ship lost nearly all power and struggled to hold its own. Growing wearier, the thought crossed Lam's mind again and again that they were crazy to think they could stop a force that had enslaved the entire civilized galaxy. But they were gaining the advantage now if they could continue to press it. He took a deep breath, flexed his hand to loosen a cramp and fought on.

"Is it done?" Kurdon asked his communications officer, his face stone-like and his voice cold.

"Yes, Exalted Kurdon. The carrier captain reports that the engines are flooding. The explosion will destroy the Tsuian fleet and half of the planet's atmosphere," replied his officer in a businesslike manner.

"Then let us return to base." Kurdon's flagship peeled away from the carrier and sped toward the light gate. Lam watched it shimmer and disappear through the light gate along with several other ships that had taken off from the carrier. Though it was obvious the Tsuians were winning, Lam was highly suspicious of what he had seen.

Lam turned to question Jern, "The leader of the Dominion is a guy named Kurdon, right?"

"That's what I learned on the destroyer. Kalen probably had something to do with the destroyer exploding, come to think of it," Jern realized.

"Well, that must have been Kurdon's flagship that just went through the light gate, along with several others."

"Do you think it's time to use this?" asked Jern, holding up the prized Emec programming card.

"I think so." Then Lam called to the fleet, "Jern and I are going to the Dominion's base planet. Follow when you're able." Starjumper pulled out of the battle and flew toward the light gate, which lay beyond the Dominion carrier.

"Look at this!" exclaimed Jern, holding out his hand. The M-stone ring was glowing more intensely than it ever had before, with so much energy it seemed to be pulsing.

"There must be a tremendous energy force nearby," commented Lam worriedly. He quickly scanned the area and yelled, "Those foul butchers! They've flooded the carrier's engines. If that thing blows here . . ."

"I suppose it's too late to disarm it," offered Jern. Lam nodded as he bit his lip in concentration. Then Jern brightened, "Can we give it a shove into the moon's gravity so it will crash there and confine the explosion?"

"Good idea," commended Lam, already swinging Starjumper toward the carrier. Lam called for help and the battle shifted to the carrier with several ships pushing against the carrier and the rest covering them. The engines of the Tsuian ships and Starjumper fired nearly full power and their blue shields glowed brightly where they pressed against the carrier's hull. The carrier did not budge at first, but then slowly and with increasing speed it inched closer to the moon. Soon the moon had it in its gravity and the giant craft fell.

Lam pulled Starjumper back toward the light gate. The fleet followed, pursued by the dogged remnants of the Dominion armada. The bolts were still flying as Lam and the Tsuians passed through the light gate, became hazy and indistinct and then became flashes of energy headed toward the Dominion base. The remaining missiles, their targets now gone, drifted into space or fell to the planet where they burned in the atmosphere. The Dominion ships did not know their enemy now raced to their base, but after regrouping, they passed the light gate and followed them.

Kurdon dropped his hand on his seat's com-link. He was still groggy from re-massing, but he did not wait.

"This is Kurdon to the palace guard," he said, his speech still slightly slurred.

"Yes, Exalted Kurdon," the answer snapped back.

"Put all hands on the ground to air defenses. Alert the patrol to guard the light gate."

"Yes, Exalted Kurdon."

Kurdon's ship descended through the clouds above his city. The sun glinted off of the metal, glass and polished stone which could be seen even from space. He stared at the viewing screen and watched his city grow closer as he spoke to the Doomen beside him.

"It will take a while to rebuild our strength," Kurdon addressed coldly. "In the meantime, we will have to finish off these Tsuians. Recall your Doomen from the planets in this septant— we will need their assistance."

Chapter Twenty-two

When Starjumper re-massed, Lam stared with blurry eyes at the viewing screen. Kurdon's flagship and the few shuttles from the carrier had not yet reached the planet. As soon as feeling returned to his hand, Lam applied thrust and began to plunge through the atmosphere.

"Look out!" warned Jern pointing to a blip appearing on the side of the screen. Starjumper rocked as bolts from a Dominion patrol ship slammed into its side.

"I think they'll be more careful when we're on Kurdon's tail," noted Lam, concentrating on closing the distance between Starjumper and Kurdon's flagship. Lam was right, the patrol ship did not fire any more for fear of hitting a Dominion ship. The ground-to-air guns remained quiet for the same reason.

"What are we going to do when we catch them?" asked Jern.

Lam's voice was quiet and cold as he replied, "There are things I have been waiting to discuss with Kurdon." Jern looked with concern at the determination on Lam's face.

Kurdon's ship had settled on the palace port. A contingency of soldiers with shoulder blasters ran to it and lined up in front of the opening port. Kurdon's personal guard stepped onto the ramp and Kurdon appeared after him. The Doomen guard walked behind him as Kurdon strode swiftly into his palace while Starjumper landed beside the flagship. Huge guns from the wall of the port were trained on Lam's ship, and the soldiers circled its portal.

Jern had abandoned his joking and pleaded with his friend, "Lam, you don't have to do this." Lam had already unstrapped and was tucking his pistol beneath his tunic. He turned off the engines and the blue shield faded along with the whine. Moving

169

to the portal, Lam's face steeled. The portal hissed open and he looked down on the sea of shoulder blasters aimed at his head. Scurvit sauntered to where the guards stood, accompanied by Kurdon's lone Doomen guard.

Scurvit grinned widely and crackled, "I trust you are surrendering yourself?"

Lam turned his head, spat, and glared at Scurvit and the soldiers. Hate swept over him like a wave. He breathed harder and his blood pounded in his ears. These were the people that destroyed Entar, and Kurdon was behind it all. It might be the last thing Lam did, but he would see Kurdon pay. The Source had led him this far, and now . . . Suddenly he realized something and turned back to Jern and asked quietly, "We did not get this far by ourselves, did we?" Jern shook his head. He looked down at Scurvit and almost pitied him and the other men who had wasted their lives in service to the Dominion.

Lam drew his breath and demanded, "I would like to speak with Kurdon." Lam's voice seemed almost gentle compared to the seething hatred he had felt a moment before. Scurvit held his arm out in a mocking welcome gesture. Lam picked up his walking stick and stepped down from the ship. When he reached the ground, several soldiers boarded the ship and took Jern prisoner.

Lam stepped up to Scurvit. Scurvit nodded at the Doomen, who swiftly ripped open Lam's tunic and disarmed him.

Scurvit shook his head and scolded Lam, "We must learn to trust each other." Scurvit nodded at two guards who grabbed Lam's arms and led him behind Scurvit into the palace. They walked through an empty hangar and into a rotunda walkway. As they descended in the lift cage, Lam was awed at the frightening glamor of the palace. Marching down the long halls, their footsteps echoed off the stone walls. Lam closed his eyes occasionally and sighed a prayer. He walked as fast as he could, leaning more heavily on his cane as his legs grew weary. Finally they halted at two massive, paneled wooden doors.

"The Exalted Kurdon is waiting for you." Scurvit motioned toward the doors. The little man seemed to be enjoying himself. "Have a nice chat." He turned and walked off, followed by the guards.

Lam stood alone in front of the doors. Placing his cold hand in his pocket for warmth, he felt the amulet Padu had given him. He remembered Padu's words: "It is an expression of our faith. You will know when the time is right to put it on." Lam smiled and decided this was the time. As he pulled it out, something else came out of his pocket and landed on the floor. It was the crude M-stone amulet that Laii had worn.

"Laii, how did you manage to slip this in here?" Lam muttered. He picked it up and slipped it over his head, along with the amulet from Padu. For a moment he stood remembering Padu and Laii, but only for a moment. Silently, the doors swung open toward him and Lam stepped back to avoid being struck by them. Seeing nothing inside the dark room, he drew a deep breath and walked in.

Once inside, he could see more easily. The floor and walls were polished black and reflected the light from red torches burning beside the huge altar on one end of the hall. Lam could see a figure standing in front of the altar, his hands folded behind his back, waiting. Taking a tentative step, the doors shut behind him. He glanced around and saw there was no turning back. Turning and proceeding to the altar, each footstep seemed to echo forever. He could hear his own breathing and even the sound of the flames flapping above the torches. The fear he had felt in the presence of Doomen was nothing like what he felt now.

When Lam reached the altar, Kurdon descended one step, but still towered above him.

"So you are Padeus' tail," mocked Kurdon. "His head is crushed—tying his tail should not be difficult."

Lam looked up at the proud, powerful figure. Along with the noise of blood in his ears and the self-accusations of "Lam, you fool!", he remembered other words he had heard: "I have a purpose to work through your life . . . by the Power . . . I am your Friend."

Lam pulled himself together and proclaimed, "You have not been having good days lately."

Kurdon's face lost any hint of mirth and then growled, "I have conquered most of the civilized galaxy, and will soon have it all. Do you think you can stop me? Everything you have experienced has been carefully planned to benefit me. You are now standing before the altar that serves as the focal point for a power greater than you could comprehend, and that power has brought you here. That power is my master, and he richly rewards those with courage enough to follow him."

Kurdon's eyes glared icily at Lam from a stony face. "You cannot defeat me. You serve a weak and cruel master." He looked at Lam's leg, supported by the walking stick and continued, "He takes strong men and cripples them. He gives them hope and then dashes it. He kills their friends and abandons them in space. Do you remember how it was to walk? Do you remember what it was like to sleep in peace? Yes, you serve a cruel master."

Kurdon's words were like barbs. Lam knew the Source was not like that, but somehow Kurdon knew the things that had hurt him the most. He looked down at his leg and then at his walking stick. He knew what to do next.

"I will show you what my master does with the crippled," declared Lam. Lam grabbed his cane with both hands and swung it with all his strength at Kurdon's midsection. Kurdon swiftly drew his metal rod from his belt to catch the blow. Their staffs collided and the crash filled the room, paining Lam's ears. He scrambled to reach the step where Kurdon stood. By this time Lam's amulets glowed fiercely and the red stones in Kurdon's breastplate also glowed.

Lam raised his cane and swung again, this time aiming for Kurdon's skull. When their rods met again, there was a crack like lightning and thunder, and sparks scattered across the polished floor. With the crash still ringing in his ears, Lam lunged toward Kurdon and threw his body weight behind a swing he hoped would connect with Kurdon's flesh, but the Dominion's ruler jumped aside with a sure step and Lam's cane hit the railing that ran up the steps to the altar. The railing's metal screeched as it bent and tore out of its stone base.

Lam hesitated a moment for a glimpse at his handiwork. *How could I have done that?* he wondered. The white hot amulet burning against his chest answered his question. The M-stones were glowing intensely, amplifying his emotional and physical energy. "I will never fail you" ran through his mind.

A footstep jerked Lam from his reverie and he swung around.

Kurdon had drawn near and stood, hands at his side, as if daring Lam to attack. Kurdon's face was expressionless, but his eyes were mocking. Lam could see that the red stones in Kurdon's breastplate were glowing as intensely as his own blue-white stones. What unnerved Lam even more were the eyes of the serpent on the altar. When Lam first entered the hall, they merely reflected the flickering torchlight; now they shone with a blood-red light of their own. Lam hesitated again. Kurdon would not invite his attack if he felt Lam might prevail. Something in Lam urged him to lunge.

Again and again Lam swung. At first he planned his blows, watching for an opening and then leaning into the attack, but as Kurdon deflected each blow, Lam's swings became rapid and wild. Kurdon's face was set in a determined expression as he deftly caught Lam's strokes and returned them with cruel force. As they dueled on the steps, Kurdon began to beat Lam down. He rained powerful strokes on Lam, forcing him to one knee as he defended himself.

The sound of the fight was like an entire army battling and with each blow the room lit up like lightning. Lam managed to regain his footing, but his hands were numb and his muscles ached. He wordlessly gasped a prayer as his throbbing arm raised his cane to deflect another blow from Kurdon who stood a step above him. Just as the weapons connected, Lam's heel slipped to the next step and he stumbled backward. Kurdon, expecting to meet more resistance, had hurled the weight of his body into the blow, so when Lam fell backward to the floor, Kurdon stumbled too.

Lam lay in agony, face up on the cold, black stone. Kurdon caught himself on the twisted railing but dropped his rod in doing so. Lam's eyes were not focusing, and he seemed dazed. Kurdon did not hesitate to press his advantage. Without stopping to pick up his rod, Kurdon leaped down the stairs to stand beside Lam's head. Raising a cleated boot above Lam's face, he prepared to crush Lam's skull. Lam saw the whole event as if in slow motion. The noise in the room seemed strangely distant, and his body unresponsive. Lam rubbed his blurry eyes and focused enough to see the boot descending. Somehow Lam managed to raise his cane, one hand on each end, to protect his head.

The move so surprised Kurdon, however, that Lam succeeded in pushing his cane against Kurdon's boot to send him sprawling. With a grunt Lam propped himself up and saw Kurdon quickly regain his footing and snatch up his rod. Lam staggered to his feet to meet Kurdon's attack and they began sparring again. Lam did not fight well this time and began to panic as Kurdon forced him to retreat up the steps, backing him against the black altar. Able only to defend himself, Lam held his staff above his head, feeling weaker with each blow Kurdon rained on him.

The Tsuian fleet had been out of the light gate only moments when the ground-to-air defenses launched bolts at them that made them scatter. A nearby defense satellite also began swiveling, trying to aim its weapons at one of the passing fighters. Moments later, the Doomen fighters began to re-mass and renew their attack.

"I don't know how much more of this I can take," cried Melena wearily to Wil. Wil was swinging the fighter out of the way of bolts and trying to maneuver the craft into position to fire at one of his elusive targets.

"I know what you mean. I'm exhausted and my hands are cramped."

The attack was more vicious than the first time. The Doomen seemed strengthened by being near their home planet. One Tsuian fighter after another was struck. Several of their shields faded dangerously.

"Do you think we should retreat?" Wil asked his sister regretfully.

"No, but I don't think we can do anything but defend ourselves. These Doomen don't seem to tire." As she spoke, a bolt from the planet slammed into the ship.

"The shield's down!" gasped Wil. "I can hardly control the ship!" Melena tried the cannon activator and found that it, too, was useless. Alarms and lights on the ship began to confirm their trouble.

Melena sank her head into her hands and cried out to the Source. There was nothing more they could do.

"What in the galaxy?" exclaimed Wil with surprise. Melena looked up and saw what surprised Wil. There were no red bolts coming from the Doomen ships; in fact, it appeared the Doomen fighters were spinning out of control.

Lam's body could endure no more. Kurdon slammed his rod against Lam's staff, and Lam's hands and arms lost their strength. The blow knocked Lam's staff out of his hands and it tumbled down the steps and skidded across the black floor. Falling against the altar in fatigue, he watched his weapon and his support roll away, echoing emptily in the dark hall.

Lam looked up in horror as Kurdon raised his staff in both hands, preparing to deal the final deadly blow. Kurdon's face was lit from beneath by the red glow of the stones as he swung massively at his defenseless victim. Somehow Lam found the will and the strength to roll aside as the blow fell. Instead of hitting Lam, Kurdon's rod slammed into the altar and chips of black stone flew from the gash.

Kurdon gasped and dropped his rod. He stood and stared in horror at the damaged stone, shocked at having desecrated his master's altar. Lam lay on the steps, catching his breath, watching. Kurdon's hands shook and he seemed immobilized with terror as the altar quivered and began to crack. Lam pulled himself up by the twisted railing and limped down the stairs as the black stone began to crumble and fall. The tremendous redstone empowered force that rained blow after blow upon Lam's M-stone strengthened cane had slammed into the altar. Perhaps the altar had also been channeling power to Kurdon and his metal rod. Now having been turned against the altar itself, Kurdon's rod had dealt a devastating concussion.

Kurdon did not move as the massive altar split. Soon the hall was filled with a rumble as from an earthquake. The carved serpent on the altar seemed to scream in pain, but it was just the sound of tearing stone. Kurdon still did not move, but his mouth opened in a wordless cry as the carving and half of the altar split away and collapsed over him. The red flames of the torches died, and the hall grew dark and silent except for the echoes of the battle.

The Le-in insisted on preparing the feast. This freed the friends of the fighter pilots to gather around and listen to their electrifying accounts of the battle and the rescues of the crippled Tsuian fighters. Lam was standing back in the shadows, leaning against Starjumper, content just to watch the others laugh and tell their stories in the glow of the fire light. He felt a hand on his shoulder and turned to see Hud's smiling face. "None of us can possibly thank you enough for all you've done," beamed Hud, leaning against Starjumper's hull beside Lam. Lam only smiled and nodded. He could hardly believe it was all over.

"Let's not forget where our true thanks belong. Without our Friend . . ." Lam choked and could say no more.

"We were right in guessing that the Doomen were not really alive," mused Hud after a few moments of similar emotions.

"You've buried all the bodies of the Doomen then?" asked Lam, shivering at the thought of what the Doomen really were.

"Yes," answered Hud quietly. "The bodies are now free to return to dust as they were meant to. I doubt most of the people in the galaxy will believe that the Doomen were evil-empowered walking corpses, but at least we don't have to worry about them anymore."

Lam thought about Hud's comment, and then asked, "Aren't you afraid though, of the force behind the Doomen?"

Hud turned to look at Lam and smiled.

"Aren't you glad you are on the right side?"

Lam laughed and rejoiced. Real joy was vibrating in Lam's soul. He then looked down to see what was tugging at his flight pants. He saw several Tsuian and Le-in children.

"Excuse me, Hud," laughed Lam. "Our discussion will have to wait. It seems I'm needed for a serious game right now."

Hud watched Lam walk off with the children running around him pretending to be fighters. "You are a chosen man," sighed Hud softly so that Lam would not hear. Hud also looked at Melena who was laughing with the others around the fires. He looked back at Lam, now losing a battle with the tiny fighter pilots, and smiled. "You'll soon discover there's more in store for you, my friend. Much more." He slapped Starjumper on her hull and walked back to the warmth of the fires.